Chase sought Mallory's gaze, intentionally holding hers. "Just tell me. Get it over with, so I can go to bed."

She lowered her lashes demurely. There was something about her Chase couldn't identify, but it tugged at him, making him want to tell her it was okay, that she could tell him anything. That at least he'd listen, even if he didn't believe her.

"Your horse, Peggy Sue, is a special animal. Legend has it that her kind can only be tamed by a chaste and innocent maid."

Chase stared at her. Something akin to a red-hot poker finished him off in the chest. He couldn't breathe. "You're a virgin," he said flatly. "Untasted, untouched, untempted."

She met his gaze again. "Oh, no, Chase. Not untempted."

Dear Reader,

Grab a front-row seat on the roller-coaster ride of falling in love. This month, Silhouette Romance offers heart-spinning thrills, including the latest must-read from THE COLTONS saga, a new enchanting SOULMATES title and even a sexy Santa!

Become a fan—if you aren't hooked already!—of THE COLTONS with the newest addition to the legendary family saga, Teresa Southwick's *Sky Full of Promise* (#1624), about a stone-hearted doctor in search of a temporary fiancée. And single men don't stay so for long in Jodi O'Donnell's BRIDGEWATER BACHELORS series. The next rugged Texan loses his solo status in *His Best Friend's Bride* (#1625).

Love is magical, and it's especially true in our wonderful SOULMATES series, which brings couples together in extraordinary ways. In DeAnna Talcott's *Her Last Chance* (#1628), virgin heiress Mallory Chevalle travels thousands of miles in search of a mythical horse—and finds her destiny in the arms of a stubborn, but irresistible rancher. And a case of amnesia reunites past lovers—but the heroine's painful secret could destroy her second chance at happiness, in Valerie Parv's *The Baron & the Bodyguard*, the latest exciting installment in THE CARRAMER LEGACY.

To get into the holiday spirit, enjoy Janet Tronstad's *Stranded with Santa* (#1626), a fun-loving romp about a rodeo megastar who gets stormbound with a beautiful young widow. Then, discover how to melt a Scrooge's heart in Moyra Tarling's *Christmas Due Date* (#1629)

I hope you enjoy these stories, and please keep in touch!

Mary-Theresa Hussey

Mary-Theresa Hussey
Senior Editor

Please address questions and book requests to:
Silhouette Reader Service
U.S.: 3010 Walden Ave., P.O. Box 1325, Buffalo, NY 14269
Canadian: P.O. Box 609, Fort Erie, Ont. L2A 5X3

Her Last Chance

DeANNA TALCOTT

SILHOUETTE *Romance*®

Published by Silhouette Books

America's Publisher of Contemporary Romance

Dedicated to the memory of Kay Landon,
who prompted me to take this magical,
mystical journey into the world of my imagination.
She is the angel sitting on my shoulder.

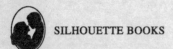 SILHOUETTE BOOKS

ISBN 0-373-19628-8

HER LAST CHANCE

This edition published by arrangement with Harlequin Books S.A.

® and TM are trademarks of Harlequin Books S.A., used under license.
Trademarks indicated with ® are registered in the United States Patent
and Trademark Office, the Canadian Trade Marks Office and in other
countries.

Visit Silhouette at www.eHarlequin.com

Printed in U.S.A.

DeANNA TALCOTT

grew up in rural Nebraska, where her love of reading was fostered in a one-room school. It was there she first dreamed of writing the kinds of books that would touch people's hearts. Her dream became a reality when *The Bachelor and the Bassinet,* a Silhouette Romance novel, won the National Readers' Choice award for Best Traditional Romance. That same book also earned a slot as a *Romantic Times* nominee for Best Traditional Romance, and was named as one of *Romantic Times'* Top Picks. DeAnna's third Silhouette Romance novel, *To Wed Again?,* also won WISRWA's Readers' Choice award for Best Traditional Romance.

DeAnna claims a retired husband, three children, two dogs and a matching pair of alley cats make her life in mid-Michigan particularly interesting. When not writing, or talking about writing, she scrounges in flea markets to indulge #1 son's quest for vintage toys, relaxes at #2 son's Eastern Michigan football and baseball games, and insists, to her daughter, that two cats simply do not need to multiply!

Narwhal, Unicorn of the Sea

When the world was young, an extraordinary horse was banished to an island that came to be known as Narwhal. The gentle white beast, with the spiral-like ivory horn growing from its forehead, multiplied and lived in harmony and happiness. People soon learned that the horn, if given freely by such a horse, would spill forth with goodness and healing powers. The horse, greatly revered, was christened "the unicorn."

Although the unicorn could only be tamed by a chaste and innocent maiden, one day a greedy landowner, discontent with his lot, captured a unicorn and forced it into servitude. A plague soon descended upon the island, and the unicorn grew sickly. A peasant, recognizing the broken spirit of the once-proud animal, chose, at great personal risk, to free it.

The unicorn fled to the hills, tossing its head in the sunshine, a rainbow at its back as it danced over bubbling spring water. In shame, the cruel landowner who had lost all of his possessions and all of his friends because of his selfishness, moved far, far away. When he was gone, peace and well-being returned, bringing the people a wealth beyond measure.

From that day forward, and for hundreds of years thereafter, a promise was made: any unicorn taken from the land, then returned to their origins, would dance with joy over the waters, blessing the people from the wellspring of life.

Chapter One

"Dagnabbit!" Chase Wells winced and sagged heavily against the back wall of the barn. Then he simply surrendered to the pain and bent over double. He gave it a good minute before he straightened or even tried to flex his leg—when he did, he promptly clamped his jaws around a swear word.

In the back of his head, he could hear his mama scolding him.

Bite your tongue, Chase Benton Wells!

He gritted his teeth so hard, the enamel actually hurt.

Just as quickly, determination rose in him like a challenge. He wasn't one to give up, never had been, never would be. He'd spent his whole life working this ranch and he'd taken his fair share of lumps. He'd fallen out of the bed of a pickup at seven, turned the tractor over when he was twelve, been gored by a bull at seventeen, and nearly drowned trying to spur his stallion across a swollen stream at twenty-three. One contrary four-year-old wasn't going to give him grief.

He intended to tame that rambunctious little mare, or die trying. She was, by far, the most ornery animal he'd ever raised. Her mama, one of his prize Morgans, had taken a fancy to one of the wild mustangs that ran through the West and jumped the fence four years ago. When he'd recovered her months later, she was in foal with the little varmint who'd later come to be known as Peggy Sue. This mare, he observed ruefully, had apparently inherited her daddy's bad temperament.

A small, lopsided grin unexpectedly dented his face, as he thought about their daily run-ins. Yesterday, Peggy Sue had left her calling card: a hoofprint on his belly, in nicely colored bruises. The day before that she bit him.

Using his shoulders, Chase pushed off the rough-sawn siding and tottered uncertainly on his one good leg. He yanked off his leather gloves and jammed them into his back pocket, before sinking his boot heel into the gritty dust of the barn floor and gingerly testing his weight. A groan immediately ripped through his lungs, and he shuttered his eyes against the unmerciful current of blue-black pain that exploded behind his eyelids.

He was getting too old for this, that's what. Thirty-four years old and hobbling around like a broken-down cowboy.

Behind him, Peggy Sue kicked the boards of her box stall. *Take that!*

Chase didn't even give her the satisfaction of looking over his shoulder; he just staggered out of the barn and into the blinding Wyoming sunshine.

He heard the hum of a car motor before he could actually focus on it. Squinting, he looked toward the house. Near the side porch of his sprawling log home, a snazzy little red convertible idled. Behind the wheel, with her blond hair floating over her shoulders, sat an angel.

He stared, smitten with disbelief.

Yup, that confirmed it. He'd died and gone to heaven. That little mare had kicked him into kingdom come.

He expected the angelic-looking woman to float out of the car, but she got out the traditional way, door and all. He started limping toward her, figuring he might as well go meet his fate. It was pretty obvious she didn't have her wings with her. Instead, she was wearing the softest, curviest white top, and sexiest little pair of jeans and sandals. She waved at him, and the bracelet on her wrist tossed off glittering sparks.

He tipped his head, offering up his best Wyoming welcome, and wondering what the heck a woman like that was doing out in the remote country of Horseshoe Falls. Sucking in a deep breath, he made a conscious effort to shake off the pain and find out.

"Hi," she called. "I hope I've got the right place. You must be Chase Wells."

"I am." He wiped his palm over his jeans, anticipating the introduction. He paused long enough to slide a lazy, assessing gaze over her. Right from the top of her windblown, tawny-streaked hair to the tips of her dainty feet and red-painted toenails.

His first impression was mind-blowing. The woman was as smooth as her flawless complexion, her moves as silky as her cultured accent. She was slender and willowy, and she carried herself with a confident air. With her chin tipped high, the mannerism wasn't quite enough to give her straight nose a snobbish tilt, but rather an implied awareness of her surroundings. Her eyes were incredibly blue— like matched sapphires—and her brows arched over them like a pair of exquisite frames.

Then she smiled—and Chase's pain ebbed and faded to a distant memory. His limp was reduced to a minor irritation. It struck him, oddly, how her mouth looked moist.

Pink. Curving in just the right places, as if she knew how to make the most of a smile—and probably a kiss.

In one insane moment, he wondered if she kissed boo-boos—because he certainly had acquired a bunch of them.

"Hello," she said, extending her hand. "I've had a terrible time. I took the wrong turn or something a few miles back." The pressure of her grasp was negligible. She dragged her long, slim fingers across his palm, the tips of her ovaled nails sliding between his thumb and forefinger as seductively as a caress. "I'm Mallory Chevalle."

Chase branded the name on his fuzzy brain and, quickly assessing her stunning attributes and the intriguing inflection of her voice, realized there was something vaguely familiar about her.

"You have a lovely home," she continued, letting her gaze drift past his shoulders to the vista of mountains to the west, then to the lush valley behind the barns, the corrals and the house. "It's more like a resort than a ranch."

"We're comfortable." Chase squinted, wondering why any woman who wore diamond studs rather than turquoise in her ears was looking for the Bar C.

She laughed, an engaging little sound that seemed to bubble right up from the depths of her soul. "I honestly don't know how you get any work done. I'd be saddling up every day for a ride."

"Working ranches don't offer up a lot of time for pleasure riding."

"That's a shame, especially when you raise such fine Morgans."

"You know about our stock?"

"Of course. I was pretty impressed with how some of your mares placed at the stock show in California."

Chase nodded, putting two and two together. His partner, Bob Llewelyn, made the rounds this time of year, training and showing in all the big Morgan shows. Bob was an affable guy, he made friends with everyone. "And you came all the way out here to check us out?"

"No…" She apologetically lifted a shoulder. "Your partner sent me."

Chase couldn't beat back his surprise.

"I told him I was looking for stock for my family's stables, and he promised I'd find just what I wanted. Um…he mentioned, too, that you've even got some stock that's part mustang. That you've worked with some of the free-roaming mustangs that have been captured and relocated."

Chase frowned and glanced back at the barn, annoyed that he hadn't taken time to close the door. It wouldn't do for her to come across that lame-brained Peggy Sue. "Yeah. I have. But what're you interested in for your stables? Specifically."

She looked like she was about to say something, then stopped. "Why don't you show me what you've got?"

Something about her answer sounded a little hollow and didn't ring true. Experience told him buyers always knew what they wanted. They either needed broodmares or a good show horse. They wanted a stud to improve their stock or a pleasure horse for their kids. He glanced at her suspiciously, not quite believing she drove hundreds of miles just to browse through the merchandise.

She paused, the hint of a frown clouding her features, darkening her eyes. "You were expecting me, weren't you?"

Chase inclined his head, vaguely wondering if he should have checked the answering machine again. At that precise moment something near his heart started vibrating. If he hadn't known better, he'd have thought this Mallory woman had created the stir.

He pulled the snap on his chest pocket and pulled out his cell phone. "Excuse me," he apologized, taking a step back and slightly turning his back.

"Chase?" his partner, Bob Llewelyn, inquired.

"Yeah?"

"Sorry, buddy. I forgot to tell you Mallory Chevalle is headed your way. Put her up for a few days, will you? Show her around, give her a good time. Her daddy's that shipping magnate, Hewitt Chevalle?" The realization hit Chase like a ton of bricks. From his peripheral vision, Chase narrowed a gaze at the woman who had politely turned away from eavesdropping on his call. "Mallory's interested in buying some stock for the family's estate in Narwhal."

"Well…thanks for the warning."

"No problem."

"She's here now."

"Oh." The word was small, precise and cautious. "The house isn't a mess, is it?"

"What do you think?" Chase snapped. "It's a ranch house, not a guest house."

Bob coughed, letting a second of strained silence slip away. "Didn't mean to inconvenience you," he said finally, "but I figured we could use at least one client who wouldn't quibble over the price."

Chase snorted. "I've got forty Morgans that need my attention. I haven't got time to serve up a little luxury, like brunch at eleven and tennis at four. Sorry."

"Well, you know," Bob went on, "the thing about Mallory is, she likes cowboy boots and leather jackets just fine. Put her to work. She won't be in the way."

"Put her to work," he repeated. "Is that before or after the beluga caviar, Brie cheese and vintage wine?"

Bob guffawed. "Chase, you got it wrong. This is one

woman that doesn't need to be waited on. She won't be any trouble at all.''

''Right.''

''Hey, I'm telling you. Money's no object, not to the Chevalles of Narwhal. They're loaded, but you'd never know it. And Mallory might be an heiress, and a hands-off woman, but she's a real fine gal to spend some time with.''

''I'll file that away for future reference,'' Chase said unpleasantly.

''Do that. Keep her happy, Chase. It'll be in the best interests of the Bar C.''

Knowing he had no other choice but to give in, Chase ended the call. Although Mallory had discreetly turned her back, Chase regretfully wondered how much of the conversation she'd heard.

She swiveled, her sandaled foot pivoting on the gravel. With her head down, she glanced up at him demurely, the corners of her almond-shaped eyes lifting slightly in amusement. ''He didn't tell you, did he?''

''My partner has a little trouble with some organizational skills. Like being on time, forwarding messages or paying the taxes when they're due. It plumb slipped his mind to warn me that you were coming to look at stock, Miss…um…Chevalle.''

''Mallory. Just call me Mallory.''

He nodded tightly. ''Narwhal,'' he said thoughtfully. ''Is that somewhere up near Monaco, or that neck of the woods?''

''Close. At least it's on that side of the ocean,'' Mallory said, fighting the urge to grin at Chase Wells's discomfort. American men were so peculiar when it came to Europeans and Old World money. They simply did not know how to handle it, how to behave or what to say. So, instead, they always swaggered a little and slipped into a ''don't mean nuthin' to me" demeanor. A perverse thought went winging through her head, and Mallory gave in to it. "Did I hear you say something about tennis? We really should play a set. I'd love to see you in your whites on the court later this afternoon."

Chase stared at her. Not one muscle in his handsome face twitched—and he did have a handsome face. A shock of Cherokee-black hair swept back from his wide forehead and feathered away from his temples. It was cropped in neat arcs over his ears, with a scruffy little fringe riding his shirt collar. He had a thick jaw, blunt chin and a mouth that just managed to wander a little higher on the right side. Beneath a slash of dark lashes, his eyes were gunmetal gray.

"Tennis? I thought you came out here to look at horses."

Mallory swallowed a giggle and carefully arranged her face for the rugged cowboy, feigning innocence. "Oh, I did. But tennis is such a great stress reliever, don't you think?"

He sucked in a deep breath, pumping his brawny chest up another intoxicating notch. Mallory could barely tear her gaze away. Considering her words, he hung his thumb over his pewter belt buckle while the toe of his boot swiped at a rock on the drive. "The thing is, ma'am, this here's Wyoming. We don't play them silly little games out here. And the only thing I got that's white is my underwear."

Mallory laughed, even as a touch of pink stained her cheeks. "Then we should get along just fine. Because I haven't had a racket in my hand for five years, and I never do brunch. The day's half gone by then, and I like to get up early."

Chase hesitated, then his mouth curled and the corners of his eyes slightly crinkled.

Mallory innocently lifted her shoulder. "Bob said you

could put me up for a week or so. Until we settle on the horses.''

Chase didn't reply. He just looked at her, his eyelids narrowed, his brow furrowed.

"I can sleep anywhere. Really."

"Mmm." He didn't sound convinced, he just kept looking at her, in that disturbing cowboy way, as if something else was going on in his head.

"If you've got an extra pillow and a blanket, I can sleep on your sofa."

He barely inclined his head.

"I promise not to be any trouble."

"Persistent little thing, aren't you?" he said finally. "Ma'am, you don't understand. This isn't a bed-and-breakfast. It isn't a resort." He rocked back on his heel, and for a flickering instant Mallory was certain she saw him grimace. "It's a business. I sell horses, I don't offer a weekend getaway at a dude ranch."

"Perfect. Because I don't want one," she said. "I want the perfect horse. I want something special and unique. For my father. And, from what Bob tells me, you have it. I'll pay well for what I want, and I guarantee I'll make this worth your while." Mallory didn't intend to sound haughty or pretentious. But she wanted the mare Bob told her about—and she felt driven to bring it home to Narwhal, where it belonged. Her father's health was failing quickly and time was of the essence. "A week," she bargained. "One week out of your life for a business deal…that's not so difficult, is it? If I don't see what I'm looking for I'll be on my way. On the other hand…"

"Yes?"

"Narwhal has a wonderful summer camp for children. One of my favorite charities is to donate horses for their riding program. Maybe you'll have something they could use. If I don't find one thing, maybe I'll find the other."

Chase, his features tightening, looked away and made that fascinating whistling sound cowboys make, by crimping his lips and blowing air between his teeth.

"I don't want to intrude. I could sleep in the bunkhouse," she offered. Then she glanced over the assortment of barns and outbuildings. "You *do* have a bunkhouse, don't you? They always have them in the movies."

He turned back, arching a disbelieving brow at her. "Yes, and I can see it now. You, and Lewt, and the rest of the boys, hanging out and playing poker and drinking beer till midnight." He drew a hand over his face, scowling down at her. "Listen, Mallory, I think it's nice that you want a good-looking little pony to take home as a souvenir. For your daddy, or your projects or whatever. But I do more than sell horses. I look for a good fit. With my animals, I make a solid match with the buyer. I've got a reputation to protect—and that means I don't sell to just anybody."

Mallory stiffened, drawing back. Her pride suffered, but self-control was necessary. She had to see that animal, she had to bring it home to her father. "I understand," she replied coolly. "But I'm not just anybody. I'm Mallory Leatrice Chevalle of Narwhal, accomplished equestrienne." She paused for emphasis. "That's horsewoman, to you. In Wyoming language." The muscle along Chase's jaw thumped, giving Mallory indescribable satisfaction. "I'm equal to any mount you offer me. And I know my horses."

A flicker of interest sparked in his steely gaze. "Really?"

"Really."

"Okay. Then you can have the guest room," Chase grudgingly allowed. "Breakfast is on the table at 6:00 a.m. The rest of the day is catch-as-catch-can. And it's nothing fancy. We do plain food and plain hard work. We'll start this afternoon, because I've got some spirited mounts I'd like to show you. In fact, we're working with one right now that you might want to take a look at.''

Chapter Two

Chase watched Mallory lean over and reach in the back seat of her flashy convertible. The subtle shift of her hips, the gentle swing of her breasts enticed him.

Bristling at his own human reaction, Chase strode over to the flatbed truck and yanked his hat off the bed, then jammed it on his head. Mallory effortlessly hauled out two small suitcases.

A smidgen of guilt niggled into his subconscious. He didn't mean to treat her poorly, but he had more to do than nursemaid an heiress on holiday. Particularly in the vague hopes she'd find some little trinket—in the nature of horse-flesh—to carry back to Narwhal.

Maybe it had been memories of his daughter, Skylar, that provoked him into agreeing to this nonsense. Since she'd been gone, he'd thought a lot about what was important, what wasn't. If this summer camp for kids was legitimate, he didn't want any regrets.

Huh. When he got up this morning, he sure never figured he'd be discussing sleeping arrangements with some European highbrow. Imagining her sacked out on his couch was a stretch. It offered up a disturbing vision that taunted…like the innocuous vulnerability of Snow White, prone, before a bevy of rough-edged, hard-talking, tobacco-spitting cowboys. It just didn't equate.

"Here. Let me help you with those," he said gruffly, coming to her side.

She half turned, a protest on her smiling lips, when he reached over and snagged the suitcases from her.

A tingle of awareness immediately buzzed through his nerve endings and over his hand. Chase grimaced, and grasped the leather handles a little tighter, dismissing the sensation. Residual effect from last week, when that blasted Peggy Sue caught his hand against the manger, he told himself.

"Thank you," Mallory said politely, stepping aside, then following him up the wide grass walkway.

Silently, he forged straight ahead. The heels of his boots made a hollow sound on each of the four steps. He jerked opened the front door and, with an elbow, propped it open.

Appearing not to notice his bad humor, Mallory stopped inside the great room, her sandals pivoting on the wide knotty-pine floorboards. "Oh, my…" She glanced up at the exposed redwood beams, then down to the fieldstone fireplace. "This is so cozy."

Chase sent her a scathing look. "Yeah, just like your typical little hunting lodge, I suppose."

The comment was apparently not lost on his guest.

"Narwhalians see no value in hunting for pleasure," she replied evenly. "We are known the world over for exquisite animals, for fine horses and stables. But legend has it that our small island became invincible when a peasant, at great risk, freed a starving unicorn from its cruel master, giving the animal back his wild heart. Because of his kindness, the peasant came to know years of comfort and good health. His children, chaste and pure of heart, befriended the unicorn and came to know prosperity. For generations, people have honored his gesture. I honor it, too.''

Chase stared at her, wondering if she was putting him on. She didn't retract a word. Not one. She simply met his gaze.

''Legends…I see,'' he said uncomfortably, but not seeing at all. ''Ah…well, beggin' your pardon, ma'am. My misunderstandin' about Narwhal and all.''

Determined to change the subject, Chase moved ahead of her and into the room. He kicked down a corner of the black-and-russet Navajo rug. The room was scattered with them. Leather furnishings, a sofa and several chairs, were arranged in front of the fireplace.

Mallory trailed a hand over the rustic willow and reed high back chairs and matching table. ''Your local artisans do incredible work,'' she murmured.

Chase brushed off the comment. ''I got it from the local discount store. If you look, you'll probably find a gold foil Made in China sticker.''

Mallory lifted her eyes, her gaze narrowing. ''You do have a lovely home, Chase, no matter how you put it together.''

Her grace and tact made him feel like a heel. It wasn't hard to explain why he felt so prickly around her, but he had to put a stop to the defensive reactions and the sharp dismissals. Since Sharon—and particularly Skylar—he'd been edgy, and short with people who didn't deserve it. ''Thanks,'' he said finally. ''The old ranch house, the one I grew up in, burned to the ground about ten years ago.''

''Oh, I'm sorry. That must have been dreadful.''

He lifted a shoulder. ''We're strong. A little like the phoenix rising from the ashes.''

Mallory brightened, her features animated, her eyes dancing with recognition. ''I know that story,'' she said, ''and I love it.''

In spite of himself, he grinned, setting the suitcases down. ''You know a lot of them. Legends about Narwhal, the Phoenix…''

''I've always been fascinated with legends and lore. I've found there's a bit of truth in many of them. Particularly for those who believe.''

The sincerity of her gaze intrigued him. ''And you believe?''

The corners of her lips lifted. ''My country is steeped in legends. Stories are handed down from generation to generation, and it has been that way for hundreds of years. I believe the storytellers were the wisest, and they have knowledge to share, if we choose to listen.''

Chase stared at her, fully aware she had not answered his question. ''Well…as for our little phoenix…we were able to rebuild the house the way we wanted.'' He gestured to the huge picture windows and the vista of foothills beyond. ''Before, that view was hidden by a coat closet, a washroom and a two-car garage.''

She smiled, inclining her head. ''Ah, that was also the way of our forefathers. Function, not beauty.''

Beauty. With Mallory the word took on new meaning. Chase shifted, trying not to stare into the baby-blue depths of her eyes, trying not to acknowledge the sexy, come-hither waves of her hair.

''The Chevalles have a home on the ocean like that,'' she continued. ''At night, the fog rolls in, and it's cold and drafty and miserable. I hate staying there. I like warm, cozy things around me.''

The craziest feeling shot through Chase's arms, as if they were incredibly empty. He imagined wrapping his arms around the woman standing next to him, giving her that warm, cozy feeling. Sharing it. In that same instant, it occurred to him that they'd be good together. Very, very good together. He hastily reached down and snatched up the suitcases, before any more goofy thoughts made Swiss cheese of his sanity. He hadn't been with a woman for more than two years, and the end of that relationship had been filled with misgivings and regret. He wasn't going that way ever again. "The guest room is nothing fancy," he said, leading the way to the stairs, "but—"

"Don't." She laid a hand on his arm, stopping him. "You keep saying that. *'It's nothing fancy.'* I didn't come out here to be entertained, or to be impressed by you or your home. I came because I knew there was something special to be found. I'm not intending to stay, Chase. More than anything, I want to get home, to my father."

The room Chase offered her was charming and rustic. Mallory carefully eased her suitcase onto the brilliant hues of a ruby-and-rust quilt. It covered the four-poster bed, the bed frame made of weathered lodgepole pine. She turned to place her cosmetic bag beside the oil lamp on the old-fashioned highboy, then paused to straighten the crocheted doily beneath it.

Chase still stood in the doorway. "If there's anything else you need…" he trailed off. "Towels, soap…"

She shook her head and turned back to the suitcase.

"Extra blankets are in the hall closet."

"Thank you." She snapped the latch on her suitcase and threw open the lid. Her nightgown was on top, and she pulled it out, tossing the silk negligee onto the pillow. The spaghetti straps clung to the quilted shams, but the ivory silk slithered down the side of the bed, as if she'd issued an invitation.

Mallory was so anxious to dig out her boots that she never gave it a second thought—until she saw Chase staring at it. The gown was out of place and she knew it.

"I should have brought flannel, yes?"

He blinked, as if disturbed from his reverie.

"It's cold out here at night, I suppose," she said.

"Cold?" He looked confused. "No, not necessarily. Not in June."

"Well, the way you were looking…at my nightwear…" she continued, lifting an innocent shoulder.

Chase cleared his throat and pulled himself off the door frame. "This is cowboy country, Mallory. We don't see many of them things hanging on the line out here."

Pursing her lips, she frowned. "The line? I don't understand."

"The clothesline. Outside, drying on the clothesline," he explained. "We do wash and wear. Denim or dress shirts, it doesn't matter. It all goes in the laundry and out on the line."

"I see. Then I shall remember not to make that mistake," she said lightly, smiling at him. "Perhaps I could hang my things in your shower instead? I wouldn't want to offend anyone."

"Yeah. Okay, I guess." Inside, Chase winced. "How about if I go fix us a bite to eat, and then we start looking at stock? You want to go home, and I don't want to keep you any longer than necessary." He glanced back at her open suitcase, where scraps of silk and satin seemed to bubble out over the top. "I keep you too long, and you may go cluttering up my bath with all those skimpy little…" Feeling like a fool, he let the sentence drift, fully aware he was too embarrassed to say the word *panties* in front of some highfalutin socialite.

Mallory pulled out a stack of knit tops, balancing them

on the palm of her hand. "Don't worry. I always travel light. I can't possibly smother you in lingerie."

Chase swallowed. Hard. His lips clamped together, and he tipped his head, backing from the door.

Mallory watched him leave, and the oddest awareness coursed through her, curling down into her middle and beyond.

It was disturbing to know that the man's bedroom would be only two doors down, and that they'd share the same bath. While she didn't expect the degree of privacy she had grown up with in Narwhal, the intimacy, the nearness of the ranch house disturbed her.

No. Chase Wells disturbed her. He had from the moment her gaze fell on him.

There was no logical explanation for her feelings. None. She'd dealt with men every day of her life, but she'd never let herself get too close to any of them. Her father had raised her after her mother had died of pneumonia at an early age, and she'd grown up around the men he'd surrounded himself with. Her background in history and international law often put her in challenging situations with businessmen who contracted with her father's shipping company. Yet none of them fascinated—or provoked feelings in her—like this brief encounter with Chase Wells had.

Chase Wells was the proverbial man's man, with shoulders as wide as wood and a stance that was daring, and devil-may-care. He had the most reckless, engaging smile, and dark, brooding eyes. His gray gaze could be as seductive as smoke or as striking as silver.

It was foolish, she knew, to even consider such things. She needed to guard her innocence, particularly until this issue with her father was settled. With his health deteriorating, he often reminded her that he expected her to run his vast shipping empire. Until then he wanted her, his only daughter, to experience freedom. Yet every day she was gone from him, she missed him terribly.

Her father, Hewitt Chevalle, was an honorable man. He chided her to be capable, not spoiled, intelligent, not dull, a peacemaker of the world, not an adversary to it. When she was strong-willed, he took full credit; when she was insufferable, he took her to task.

Yes, Chase Wells would sell her the horse she wanted for her father and then send her on her way. Her family's estate, situated on the meadow where the legend claimed the unicorn once frolicked in Narwhal, was a hallowed place, with a maze of freshwater springs and flower-laden glens. Mallory was convinced that if she could bring one of the gifted animals back to its origins, her father, as caretaker, would experience relief from his debilitating disease—and she would be freed from the responsibility of running the gargantuan shipping fleet. If her father experienced respite for even a short period of time, it would be a blessing.

Chase Wells, without even knowing it, could have the solution to her problem. He may have affected her, in some strange and obtuse way that she didn't understand, but she would rise above it. She had to rise above it.

She would smile at him, gently, and win him over. It was very easy, really. All she had to do was put her mind to it. She had no other choice—because time, and her father's health—were slipping away.

Chase fed her tomato soup and grilled cheese sandwiches, and it was delicious, all of it.

"I suppose Bob told you none of the stock he's showing is for sale," he warned, rising from the table to clear away their emptied soup bowls. "Julep's TeaRose is garnering so much attention right now, we'd be crazy to sell her. As for the other two—Ruger's Opal and Ruger's Delight—they both have offers pending.''

Mallory picked up their paper napkins and wadded them together, inordinately conscious of the way Chase moved. ''I'm not necessarily interested in show stock,'' she said carefully. ''What garners interest in the world of show does not interest me.''

He waggled a brow at her, as if he didn't believe a word she said.

''I'm more interested in stock for personal reasons,'' she explained. ''As I said, I'd like to get my father something special. The idea of bringing him home an animal with mustang blood fascinates me.''

A dagger of emotion thrust at Chase's heart, then twisted painfully. Skylar had loved Peggy Sue's wild beauty, she had related to the mare with childlike trust. ''I suppose your father has dozens of Thoroughbreds.''

Her laugh was tinged with embarrassment. ''His stock is dwindling,'' she confided. ''I keep confiscating them for the children's summer camps. But he never refuses me.''

''So you're spoiled.''

''Of course. Aren't only children supposed to be?''

Reminders of Skylar—the way she wheedled to get what she wanted, the lilt of her voice, the tilt of her eyes—torpedoed through his mind. ''I don't know,'' he said stiffly, ''I've got a working ranch here—I don't dawdle around, indulging kids.''

She sighed. ''You should. It's a delightful pastime. And I don't regret it. Not one bit. Of course, I'll admit my father's estate lends itself to my purposes,'' she said. ''It's *c'alle dunois denoire et Legina de Latoix.*''

''Excuse me?''

''In your language it would translate to Valley of the Lost Legends. There are thousands of acres. Meadows as far as the eye can see, pools of fresh springwaters. And it's protected by mountains on all sides.''

"Sounds like Wyoming, ma'am.''

"Not quite. To the west, beyond the tallest of those mountains, is the Atlantic Ocean.''

"You got me there.'' Chase felt himself smile as he imagined putting one of his Morgans out to pasture, in a place that Mallory Chevalle described as if it were this side of heaven. "I imagine we'll find you something to take back to your valley. My hands are out mending fence, but Lewt's saddling up a couple of three-year-olds for you to look at. We can head down to the corral any time you're ready.''

"I'm ready now,'' she said, standing. He reached for the dirty napkins she still had wadded in her hand, but she moved them out of his grasp, avoiding contact with him. "I'm perfectly capable of putting trash in the receptacle. Thank you for lunch,'' she added, picking up his water glass and hers.

"Bob said I could put you to work,'' Chase commented, "but I don't think he meant it. In the same sentence, he warned me to treat you well.''

Mallory grinned. "He did? He's such a nice guy. I took a liking to him right away.''

Envy inexplicably welled in Chase. "Yeah. Bob's a guy you can count on.''

"If I could choose a big brother, I would choose him,'' she declared. "That's how I think of him. Like a big, wonderful friend.''

Big brother? Wonderful friend? Apparently there had been nothing between them, and Bob was a lady's man, for sure.

Relief rumbled through his chest. He didn't know why. It shouldn't even matter, not after Sharon. "Come on,'' he said, giving the table a hit-or-miss job with the dishcloth, "let me show you some good Morgan stock."

Mallory smiled eagerly over at him. "I can't wait."

It was a killer smile, and it crimped something in the region of Chase's heart.

They left the dishes in the sink, and headed out for the corral. Lewt, the oldest, the goofiest, of his hired hands, had saddled a bay filly he'd dubbed Jellybean. Well into his seventies, Lewt spent his time puttering around the horses. Another mount, a chestnut gelding named Lucifer, was tethered to the hitching post.

"Lewt, meet our guest..." Chase stalled, reluctant to introduce her as Mallory Chevalle, heiress of Chevalle Shipping. "She's interested in some good bloodlines."

"Ma'am." Lewt tipped his hat.

Mallory shook his gnarled, arthritic hand. "Hello. You must be happy, Lewt, to spend your days out here, with horses like these."

Lewt's eyes crinkled. "I am, ma'am. And I got me a nice piece of horseflesh here, if you will." He affectionately slapped Jellybean's neck.

"Ruger's Rose of Sharon," Chase explained, "otherwise known as Jellybean."

"Jellybean?"

Lewt reached over to move her forelock aside. Mallory leaned closer, her gaze riveted on Jellybean's forehead. Instead of a star, the mare had three small spots, all connected, and reminiscent of jelly beans.

"She's beautiful," Mallory said, her shoulders sagging as she allowed the horse to nuzzle her hand.

From the corner of his eye, Chase watched Mallory carefully.

Mallory had inherited the hands of an aristocrat, he allowed. Either that or the Chevalle wealth had shaped them.

Her knuckles were slim, the bones of her wrist, delicate. Long, tapered fingers moved in harmony, making each move effortless, engaging.

As Lewt moved aside, Chase watched in fascination while she ran her hands over Jellybean's head, her neck and down her withers, all the while crooning to her. Soft, lulling endearments that came from the back of her throat, her chest.

The woman was amazing. Maybe she really did know something about horses.

Mallory confidently leaned from the waist and slid her hand down Jellybean's leg, pausing at her fetlock, then lifting her hoof to examine it.

Jellybean obliged, but Chase was more intent on the way Mallory's tiny white top pulled from the back of her jeans. It fit her like a second skin, curving at the arch of her lower back, dipping into the depression that accommodated her spine. As she bent, the sleeves pulled against her arms, straining the seams in fine lines across her shoulders. Stretched thin, the knit revealed the two thin straps of her bra and the hook closure in the middle of her back. The suggestion of her intimate apparel made Chase shift uncomfortably. In his mind's eye, he saw that silky thing draped across the bed. He thought about her offhand comment, about smothering him in lingerie.

Damn, it'd be a helluva way to go.

Mallory dropped the horse's hoof, and in the back of Chase's mind, it sounded like a punctuation mark exploding in the soft dirt.

"Hard, firm, well muscled," Mallory breathlessly approved.

Chase blanched, quickly rearranging his features before Mallory lifted her innocent face to his. "All that, and more," he muttered under his breath. "Here. Let me take her out for you," he said, reaching for the reins. "See what you think."

The fact was he needed to keep his hands, his thoughts, busy. The woman riled him in ways he couldn't fathom. Sliding the toe of his boot into the stirrup, Chase threw his leg over the saddle, grateful for the ease of movement, the stretch of his jeans. Jellybean nervously sidestepped; Lewt and Mallory both backed away.

He nudged the filly into a wide canter around the arena, taking the edge off her high-strung temperament. He put her through her paces, figure eights, reining her in from a trot to a walk.

Mallory and Lewt had moved outside the corral, and their arms hung over the top rail. Periodically, Chase saw Mallory incline her head nearer Lewt's in conversation. He wondered, vaguely, what she said.

He pulled up before them, and arched a brow at her.

"She throws her head a little at every command, doesn't she?" Mallory replied to his unasked question.

Chase stared at her, definitely deflated.

"Yup," Lewt agreed mildly, propping the sole of his boot on the bottom rail as he spat into the dirt, "reckon she does. Never really noticed it until Mallory here pointed it out."

Chase felt like the value of his stock had plummeted. Jellybean was the perfect horse for Mallory. He smiled through gritted teeth. "Let's take a look at Lucifer," he suggested.

But Lucifer, Mallory decided, had a slight inclination to wring his tail. Barely noticeable, of course. But it was apparent to her discerning eyes. To Chase's consternation, Lewt agreed.

While Lewt led both animals back to the barns, Chase brought out Topaz. The filly worked beautifully, her agility to turn corners and stop on a dime her finest feature. When Mallory asked to ride her, Chase puffed up a little, figuring he'd made a match. An hour later he was planning a farewell breakfast, content he'd soon be sending the woman back to Narwhal, where she belonged. When she clambered down from the saddle, she offered Chase the reins and declared Topaz was remarkable, truly remarkable, but a little delicate in the withers. Especially for her father.

"Delicate in the withers?" he'd repeated dumbly, as visions of his buttermilk pancakes took flight.

"Perhaps a sturdier horse," Mallory remarked idly, scratching Topaz behind the ears, then stroking her forehead.

His answer to that was Stretch, three years old, sixteen hands and still growing.

Too big, she declared.

Spinner, a five-year-old mare.

Calf-hocked, she announced.

Derby, a five-year-old stallion.

Bench-kneed, she decreed.

Exasperated, Chase scowled down at the impossibly beautiful woman. She was the pickiest lady he'd ever met in his whole life. His stock was nationally acclaimed, for crying out loud. The imperfections she was tossing out were slight, barely a notch short of perfect.

Chase snagged a deep breath, determined to sell Mallory a pony, or die trying. "You know, I've got this stunning black mare—"

Mallory threw up her hands in protest. "Oh! No. Absolutely not. I had a black gelding once, and that horse was the trial of my life. Dark as the devil he was. I vowed I'd never have another in the stable."

He nodded slowly, thoughtfully. "You know, ma'am, I can't quite get a handle on what you're looking for."

"Oh, I'll know it when I see it," she said, her voice rising with conviction.

"You sure you didn't get this Bar C stock mixed up with something else you saw out in California?" he said doubtfully.

"Certainly not."

"But there's been nothing that's interested you at all today," he complained, wearily glancing to the west, to the setting sun.

"I just haven't found it yet. I'm looking for something special," she reiterated. "Something unusual and spunky. It can be less than perfect, but the overall qualities have to be so unique that they make this horse an unforgettable animal. A different kind of horse. Something not of this world."

Chase didn't hear the last sentence. He was thinking of Peggy Sue, the pariah who had head-butted him against the wall this morning. Now, there was an unforgettable animal for you. The four-year-old was more than unique, she was a minefield of imperfections—and he'd be switched if he'd show Mallory that contrary little mare.

His reputation would go to hell in a handbasket. He'd be a laughingstock from one end of the country to the other. No matter what, he had to keep her away from Peggy Sue. "We'll find you something special, Mallory. I guarantee it."

Chapter Three

With her hands in six inches of dishwater, Mallory stared dismally out the kitchen window, at the bloodred sunset, and wondered if the animal Bob Llewelyn described to her—the one with "mustang" blood running through its veins—honestly did exist. She couldn't come right out and ask, for fear her questions would arouse suspicion. Had Bob been toying with her? Had he sent her on what Americans called 'a wild-goose chase'?

It had been three grueling days, and Chase had shown her more than two dozen Morgans. Not one of those animals was the one she wanted to see. She'd hinted that she might purchase three docile animals for the camp—but that was just to keep Chase pacified.

As for buying a horse for her father—or returning it to her father's estate—she was running out of excuses. And Chase was running out of patience.

Of course, her stay wasn't all bad, she acknowledged, running the tip of her finger around the rim of Chase's coffee cup and reminding herself how his sensuous mouth had pressed against the rim only an hour earlier.

The steam from his coffee softened his rough-carved features and made his gray eyes go misty. For one heart-stopping moment during dinner tonight, she lost herself to that gaze. Chase Wells did have the most fascinating way of looking at her over a coffee cup, of following her every move with his eyes. Eyes that crinkled at the corners, and eased up into companionable crescents when he was relaxed. It was an intimacy unlike anything she'd ever experienced.

Not even in the most romantic setting, nor over the most expensive bottle of wine.

She vaguely wondered if that feeling was…*desire*. If so, she'd have to put a stop to it. She couldn't afford to become emotionally attached. Not now. Not when she was this close to getting what she wanted.

She heard the back door slam and looked over her shoulder. Chase's face was contorted with pain, and he had a handkerchief wadded against the back of his hand. Mallory dropped the coffee cup back into the dishwater and grabbed a tea towel.

"What did you do?" she asked, moving toward him.

Chase looked up, apparently surprised she was still in the kitchen. "Oh, I…um—" he grimaced, peeling the bloody handkerchief away from his hand "—got my hand caught in one of the stall doors. Stupid of me."

Mallory blinked.

Again?

Chase Wells may have been one of the most ruggedly handsome men she'd ever met, but he was also one of the clumsiest. Yesterday, he tripped over a feed bucket and twisted his ankle. The day before he got tangled in a loose cinch strap and caught his shoulder on the tack-room door.

His house was a virtual potpourri of medical supplies. She was constantly moving gauze bandages, Ace bandages, ice packs, heating pads, iodine and antiseptics out of the way.

"Let me see," she said, peering down at the damage. "You did this in a door?" she asked skeptically.

"Oh…uh…one of the horses got a little feisty, is all. We both went for the door at the same time."

"Looks like the horse won," she said dryly, her fingers carefully circling thick bones in his wrist as she led him over to the double sink. "We better wash it off and get some antiseptic," she advised, automatically turning on the faucet and putting his hand beneath the running water. The warmth of his flesh and the icy-cold rush of water aroused a strange sensation in her middle.

"I'm fine. It's just a little old scrape," he groused, resisting her ministrations.

She looked up at him from beneath lowered lashes. "I'm not trying to hurt you."

"I know. But—"

"Yes?"

"I don't need a nursemaid," he ground out.

Mallory paused and imperceptibly pulled back. "Oh, really?" He winced as she went right ahead and examined his four scraped knuckles and the deep, ragged scratches. Without offering one nuance of sympathy, she reached for the bottle of hydrogen peroxide and poured a generous amount over his wounds. "Then I promise not to," she said, leaving him to drip dry in the sink as she went to find the gauze bandages.

When she returned, he was staring thoughtfully at the tepid dishwater in the other side of the sink. "You weren't washing dishes, were you?"

"As a matter of fact, yes." She patted his hand dry with

the hand towel before slathering ointment on his scrapes. "I consider it a fair exchange for dinner."

"Right. I'll bet you've never had meat loaf in your whole life."

Her lips twitched, and she tried not to laugh. She gently wound a length of gauze over his knuckles, but she could feel his eyes on her and it was disconcerting. "No," she said finally, "I was raised on escargot, lobster with drawn butter and roast duck with orange sauce."

"Figures."

Sighing, she rolled her eyes, then tied off the bandage and tossed the gauze on the counter. "You don't like me very much, do you."

"Not true. I think you're the nicest little millionaire—or is that millionairess?—I've ever met."

She looked at him. "Chase," she said finally, her hand fluttering to his arm, "is it really the money? Does it make you uncomfortable?"

Chase's mouth went dry. He fumbled with a dozen different answers. None of them would do. The fact was Mallory had been nothing but pleasant. She laughed and the world smiled. She touched him and his heart yammered in his chest.

He looked down at the hand across his forearm.

He couldn't tell her *that* was how she made him feel. This constant yammering, whenever she was near, whenever he heard her voice or her laugh.

"I suppose I owe you an apology. Maybe I'm a little inexperienced handling someone of your caliber."

Mallory's eyes widened in mock horror. "Handling my...caliber? That does have something to do with guns, doesn't it? I'm not that explosive, am I?"

Chase's mouth curled. "Honey, you are one pistol packin' mama."

"What?"

"An expression," he said quickly. "An American expression. For someone who knows how to get what she wants. A little spitfire, someone unpredictable and maybe a little tough."

"You think I'm...*tough*...like meat?"

His eyes moved over her lips, and he wondered, insanely, what it would be like to nibble the softness he saw there. "No, not a piece of meat, not at all. All I see is...nice," he revised. "Tough, as in...determined. Yes, determined, I'll give you that."

"Mmm. You make that 'pistol packin' mama' thing sound...desirable."

Desirable. Not a word choice he needed to hear. Chase hesitated, painfully aware they'd moved imperceptibly closer to each other. His hip was against the countertop; hers was, too. Their bodies seemed to move with a will of their own, leaning, straining nearer. His breathing was shallow, his nerve endings tingled with anticipation.

It would only take one move.

One.

He vaguely wondered if, in Narwhal, they beheaded red-blooded American men for compromising unmarried women?

It just might be worth it.

Mallory drew a deep, cleansing breath, and Chase noticed it was just enough to make her breasts shudder beneath her silky white top.

So. The heady game they were playing was getting to her, too.

"It is desirable," he said huskily. "It's also sexy as hell."

Her eyes widened, as if she was startled and taken completely off guard by the suggestive comment.

"I have to finish the coffee cups," she said abruptly, turning back to the sink and plunging her hands into the dishwater. "Then I'll take a walk before it gets dark and get a little fresh air. Will you join me?"

Chase stared at her profile. The upturned nose, the graceful curve of her jaw. No. Absolutely not. Being in the dark, with a little moonlight and few freckles of stars in a blue-black sky, with a woman like Mallory—a woman who made his hands itch and his blood pound—was an invitation to trouble. "Nah," he said, brushing aside the invitation. "Go ahead. I've got some reading to catch up on."

Mallory tossed the coffee cups in the dish drainer and pulled the plug on the sink. "You're sure?"

"Yeah."

A hint of disappointment clouded her features.

She probably wasn't used to being rejected, he thought irritably as he reached for last week's stock market analysis. Either that or she liked to call the shots on everything, even a tumble through the sheets.

Yet, when she strolled out the back door and into the gathering dusk, it was he who experienced the greatest regret.

Chase couldn't concentrate; nothing he'd read made any sense. Mallory was probably fine, but he shouldn't have let her go out by herself. He glanced at the clock. She'd been gone almost an hour, and it was dark. Maybe she'd started talking to one of the hands; they followed her like lapdogs whenever they had the chance. Gabe, a fresh-faced twenty-year-old, loved to brag to her about his bull-riding exploits. Tony, with a couple of drops of Spanish blood running through his veins, had started wearing clean shirts and peppering his sentences with "*señorita*" every time she was near—as if he'd been raised across the border instead of in Boise.

Tossing the paperwork on the table, he stretched his legs, crossing one booted foot over the other. He may as well admit it, the woman was wreaking havoc with his senses and with his life. When she went home, he imagined he and his ranch hands would feel as if someone had taken the plug out of the fourteen-karat sunshine she seemed to spread.

She sure knew her horses, he'd give her that. She may have claimed she didn't want blue-ribbon horseflesh, but all her petty criticisms said otherwise. He grinned, remembering her lame excuse for not wanting Pritchett, the last mare he'd offered her.

Her ears were just a little "too pointy." Yep. Pointy ears would get you every time.

Chase flexed his hand and studied the bandage, remembering the way Mallory's fingers brushed against the sensitive spot inside his wrist as she examined his palm. His flesh still tingled, nearly blotting out all the pain.

Huh. The way Peggy Sue was having at him, she made him look like a beat-up cowpoke who didn't have one lick of horse sense. Yesterday she'd stomped on his instep, the day before she'd charged him, catching his shoulder against the wall. The duplicitous little vixen had astounding strength, even though she was so sickly, most days she could barely hold her head up. It was time to make a decision about what to do with her—and the sooner the better. She was beginning to be a risk, even a liability. His reasons for keeping her were beginning to dwindle and fade.

He flexed his hand again and grimaced. He didn't know why he was spending so much of his time thinking about Mallory, because it was Peggy Sue who was leaving her mark on him.

Painfully he hauled himself out of the chair and dragged his weary body over to the door. Snagging his hat from the peg, he pulled it low over his eyes. "Time to find the little woman," he muttered.

The moment he stepped out on the back porch and saw that the sliding door to the east barn had been pushed open, a feeling of dread washed over him. The overhead light inside the barn was on. He immediately forgot his pain, and his boot heels barely hit the stair treads as he picked up the pace.

The moment he slipped inside the barn he knew. He could hear Mallory's soft, crooning voice. He heard Peggy Sue whicker in answer. His heart did a double-time dance in his chest, and his blood went cold.

If anything happened to her...

The door to Peggy Sue's stall was open. Chase's knees went weak.

Barely breathing, he inched down the alleyway, until he was even with her stall.

Peggy Sue immediately tossed her magnificent white head, going wild-eyed, as her nose curled to expose bared teeth. The filly, even though she was on the small side, carried herself with a regal, haughty stature. Her alabaster coat faded into steel gray dappling over her rump. Her long mane and tail, also white, was tangled and dirty.

"Whoa, baby, what's the matter?" Mallory murmured. With her back to Chase, she stood at Peggy Sue's withers, and ran a hand down her neck. In her opposite hand she held a currycomb.

"Mallory," Chase said quietly, "get out of that stall now."

Mallory whirled, surprised by his entrance. "I found her, Chase," she said breathlessly, her face animated. "The one I want. This is it! This is the horse I've been looking for!"

Behind her, Peggy Sue startled, her front feet coming a foot off the ground.

"Mallory, I said get out of that stall. Now."

Mallory lost her balance and stumbled as Peggy Sue bumped her shoulders, her back. But Mallory, unfazed, squared off, planting her feet. "She's wonderful, she's spirited, she's—"

"She's going to kill you. Now, get out."

Mallory's eyes flashed and she straightened. "Don't be silly," she laughed. "I don't care what this horse costs. I have to have her. She's all I've ever imagined—and more."

Chase's muscles tensed. "You don't know what you're dealing with, Mallory."

"Oh, but I do," she said, leaning back and affectionately sinking her shoulder blades against Peggy Sue's neck. Chase's eyes briefly shuttered closed, willing the animal not to swing around and take a sizable bite out of her. "This horse is the thing legends are made of," she said, her voiced filled with awe. "She's a descendant of European stock. Her neck. Her head. Her coloring."

"That horse," Chase warned, his voice low, the cadence carefully measured, "is the meanest, orneriest she-devil this side of the Mississippi. She's got mixed blood in her. Mustang and Morgan. And she's not for sale. She's sick and mean and crazy. Now, either you get out of that stall, or I'm taking you out."

Mallory's face fell. "Chase, she's sick...I can see that...but this animal's spirit..."

"Mallory, I'm warning you."

She stared at him, then she tried a different tack. "Chase, she'll have the best vets! The best of everything. I'll see to it. Hey, girl, when I get you home..." She playfully slapped Peggy Sue on the shoulder.

Peggy Sue jumped, a dangerous whicker rumbling through her gaunt white sides.

"Don't," Chase spat, clenching his hands. "You're going to spook her, and then there'll be hell to pay." He stepped one foot inside the stall.

Peggy Sue whirled her great head in his direction, as if daring him. The motion knocked Mallory off her planted feet, and the currycomb sailed across the stall.

"Mallory, for your own safety and well-being—"

Peggy Sue laid her ears back, giving the illusion that two flat wings flanked her forelock. The knotty protrusion on her forehead was exposed, and it vaguely resembled a devil's horn. Chase had nightmares about her goring him with it. The vet said he didn't think the bone malformation caused her pain—yet pain was the only logical explanation for the mare's rages, her unpredictable behavior. Ever since Skylar had died...

As if reading his mind, Peggy Sue's eyes went hard, glassy, as she fixed her relentless gaze on him.

Chase drew a deep, cleansing breath and experimentally moved his shoulder. He had firsthand knowledge that Peggy Sue could go berserk before either of them could bat an eyelash. He prayed for the strength to whisk Mallory away. God knows, the horse *could* kill her.

He took another step, this time on his bad leg, the one she'd kicked the bejeebers out of a week ago.

Mallory looked up at Peggy Sue's unforgiving countenance. The shadow of a doubt immediately crossed her brow. "All right, all right," she said quickly. "I'll fill her grain bucket and then..." Mallory moved to the front of the stall, leaving the space between Peggy Sue and Chase wide open.

Peggy Sue saw the moment as an opportunity. The muscles in her neck and her shoulders twitched with anticipation. She pawed the ground and lowered her head.

"Easy, girl," Chase intoned, lifting a hand.

Pivoting on her hind legs, Peggy Sue reared four feet off the ground. Mallory gasped, but held fast, instinctively putting her hand up to catch Peggy Sue's halter.

Peggy Sue snorted, shouldering Mallory aside, so she could have at Chase. She faced him, blind with rage, as she cornered Mallory at the back of the stall.

Chase dashed forward, concerned Mallory would fall victim to Peggy Sue's slashing hooves. The animal was deadly. He'd have to have her put down; she wasn't right.

He moved toward the manger, and Peggy Sue's rump swung away from Mallory as she followed him.

"Mallory, get out of the corner," he ordered. "Now!"

Mallory slipped around Peggy Sue, and Chase moved farther into the stall so Mallory could exit. "Are you all right?"

"Of course I'm all right. I'm fine! You don't understand," she said behind him. "She'd never hurt me. It's her nature, she knows I'm—"

Looking over his shoulder at Mallory, Chase never saw it coming. But he heard Peggy Sue whirl before her two rock-hard hooves caught his side and propelled him against the wall. In the recesses of his mind, he heard Mallory scream—and in one insane flash of recognition he felt inordinately grateful it was he who had taken the blow. The air whooshed out of him, collapsing his lungs into aching sacks of tissue.

It was then he knew the ultimate meaning of "being hit by a two-by-four." The pine walls of Peggy Sue's stall smashed against his backside; he slowly slithered down them, as if the bones had been removed from his body, and he sank onto the straw-covered floor in a mangled blob of body parts.

"Chase! Chase!"

His hearing had been rearranged; it was if the sounds were coming from deep inside his head. His eyes fastened on the strangest things—a loose nail protruding from the manger, a small split in Peggy Sue's hoof, the dainty toe of Mallory's boot, the curve of her jeans as they stretched over her bent knee. He lay there, wondering if he was breathing, wondering if that was what made him hurt so much.

"Chase, answer me!"

Over the scent of straw and manure and horseflesh, he smelled her sweet perfume. Wildflowers on a summer day. The overhead light circled a mane of blond hair, and he looked, dumbly, into the most angelic face he'd ever seen.

"You are so beautiful," he mumbled thickly, tasting blood, his teeth feeling loose in his head. He heard the shrill, agonizing warning of a horse named Peggy Sue.

Mallory looked up and over her shoulder at the monstrous beast that pawed the air above them. "We've got to get you out of here," she said, slipping her hands beneath his armpits and dragging him from the stall. She dumped him on the hard-packed dirt floor.

His eyes shut, he heard the gate close with a bang and the latch pin sliding into the slot. He lay there, fading in and out of consciousness.

Peggy Sue continued to fuss, her back hooves splintering the boards of her box stall. He'd have to patch it up again. My God, that was one contrary horse.

He felt hands flutter over him, touching him. Sliding down his arms, his legs. Loosening his belt, unsnapping his shirt. For a moment, Chase wondered if these were heavenly ministrations. Maybe someone was putting him back together. It didn't matter, it was glorious and comforting. Whatever was happening kindled a tingling that surfaced through the pain. He wanted more of it. He didn't want it to stop.

He struggled to open his eyes. Colors blurred together in a haze of pain and pleasure. Focusing on a full, sensuous mouth, he vaguely recognized lips that belonged to Mallory. For a moment that surprised him, and he wondered what had happened to Sharon, his ex-wife. She should have been yelling at him by now.

"Talk to me," Mallory whispered, her hands stirring anxiously over his chest, his shoulders, his neck. "Tell me you're okay. Talk to me," she implored. "Say something. Anything."

He opened his mouth but only coughed, pitifully strangling on a rush of air.

"I'm so sorry. I should have known." Her voice caught as she stroked his temple, his cheek. "What can I do? Tell me."

Chase went all sappy inside, then he said the first idiotic thing that went zinging through his muddled head. "Could you…could you…kiss it and make it better?" he mumbled.

She stared at him for a split second before swiveling a glance up at that idiotic horse, Peggy Sue, who was locked inside the box stall. For a moment it appeared indecision raged inside Mallory's head, then her lips swooped down over his, covering them with sweet, sweet heat. Fireworks exploded behind his eyelids…and he knew he'd died and gone to cowboy heaven.

Chapter Four

Chase faded into unconsciousness. His breathing was shallow and labored. Fear clutched Mallory, and she bent over him, scrambling to lift his wrist, to measure his pulse. Nothing. She couldn't find it, she couldn't feel anything but the heavy weight of limp muscle and bone.

As she put an ear to Chase's chest, the pearl snap buttons on his shirt grazed her cheek and the scent of his pine after-shave tormented her senses. Heat emanated from his still body. When Mallory recognized the steady thrum of his heartbeat, her eyes fluttered closed and she lay there, her head on his chest, her arms twined possessively over his shoulders. She lost herself in the reverberation that spiraled right down into her soul and gave her comfort. She basked in the nearness, the warmth of his physical body.

But, she sternly reminded herself, she shouldn't be feeling these things, she shouldn't even be touching him in such an intimate manner.

Yet what if she'd lost him? What if…?

Behind the locked gate, Peggy Sue emitted an anguished scream.

Startled, Mallory lifted her head and looked up at the unicorn's tormented features. Just as quickly, sympathy rushed through her veins. "It had to be done," she explained hastily. "It was only a kiss, after all. A kiss and concern. Nothing more."

Peggy Sue reared, ramming the gate with her chest.

"Stop it!" Mallory warned, bending from the waist and away from Chase. "Sometimes compromises have to be made."

Peggy Sue defiantly shook her great head.

"But he doesn't know!" Mallory implored. "And if anything happened to him…" She let the statement drift as a strange, unrecognized emptiness filled her. "I don't know if we'd ever get you home again. I don't. Really."

Peggy Sue fidgeted, whickering nervously.

"And well you should be worried," she chided. "Look what you've done to him!" Mallory cupped a hand under Chase's neck and tried to raise his head. His eyelashes didn't even flutter.

"Chase?" she whispered. "Can you hear me?" His head lolled to one side, and the sandpaper-rough texture of his beard scraped against the inside of her wrist. How could a man so big, so strong, be felled so quickly? She calculated the implications of his injuries, and her blood ran cold. "It's okay," she almost pleaded, shaking him, silently begging him to rouse. "You just…you just got the wind knocked out of you. That's all. We'll get you to the doctor and—"

She heard the impatient staccato of footfalls behind her, but she couldn't tear her gaze from Chase.

"What in blue blazes…?" Lewt's gravelly voice demanded.

The three cowboys stopped in their tracks, taking in the carnage.

"Holy Mary, Mother of God," Tony supplicated, crossing himself, "protect us from the beast."

"Hell's bells." Gabe gulped. "She finally kilt him."

"Always said it was gonna happen," Lewt remarked grimly, turning his head to let a stream of tobacco juice fly over his shoulder. "Figured that horse'd be the death of him."

"No one killed him," Mallory denied hotly, straightening, and pulling away from Chase's side. Her knees, resting on the hard-packed ground, butted him in the ribs.

Chase groaned, writhing in the dirt.

"A miracle," Tony breathed, lifting his eyes heavenward.

Lewt hobbled forward, dropping down on his arthritic knee, on the other side of Chase. "Be damned if he ain't still breathing."

"Of course he's still breathing," Mallory exclaimed. "He startled the horse and she kicked him—but it was an accident!"

Lewt lifted his grizzled features, his faded blue eyes meeting hers. "Round that animal, ain't nuthin' an accident," he said.

Mallory saw insight in his gaze and recoiled from it. She couldn't deal with it now. "Help me get him up, Lewt. Help me get him to the doctor."

Chase hunched on the examining table, his chin resting on his chest, his eyes scrunched closed, as the doctor studied the X rays.

Mallory felt guilty as sin. She should have known there'd be friction between Peggy Sue and Chase. She should have at least suspected.

She glanced at Chase worriedly. It was three in the morning, and Chase hadn't uttered two coherent sentences since they'd brought him into the hospital. He was strangely silent, but the emergency room staff thought that was because of his concussion. At least he wasn't rambling about angels and pillow-top mattresses anymore.

"You're going to need some time to heal," the doctor announced.

Chase grunted.

"A mild concussion. Broke one rib and cracked another. And you got a heckuva laceration. What'd you put those horseshoes in with? Staples?" The doctor hesitated, turning the X ray another direction. "Hurt much?"

"Only…when I…breathe," Chase ground out.

"Mmm. Nice thing about that," the doctor said, seemingly unconcerned, "it reminds you you're still alive. I've seen guys take a blow like this to the heart and they end up on a marble slab, singing in the heavenly chorus. I'd say you're one lucky man."

Chase nodded. "Luck—iest damn man…in the…world," he said, grimacing.

"Can't do a thing but tape up that laceration and send you home. Sorry, buddy." The doctor tossed the X rays onto the counter and pivoted on his heel. "I know you like a little risk in your life, Chase, but in my professional opinion you'd better think this one over." Chase lifted his head to say something; the doctor kept talking. "I know, I know. We've talked about this before. But sometimes you gotta cut your losses. This might be one of those times."

Chase grunted again and made an effort to straighten.

"I'll send Josie in. She'll get you fixed up." He extended his hand, and Chase grasped it like a lifeline. The doctor didn't seem to notice. "Take care. Oh, and—" he glanced over at Mallory, giving her a broad wink "—nice to meet you, Mallory. Keep him amused, but see that he doesn't laugh too much with these injuries of his, will you?''

Josie worked her wonders with the gauze dressing, lacing him up like a drum as she secured the five-by-nine-inch pad. She pinned Mallory with a no-nonsense look. "He'll need some help for a while, getting his clothes off and on, that sort of thing." Mallory shifted uncomfortably. "And the man's not going to be as flexible as he once was, so you'll probably have to help him in and out of bed for a few days."

The idea of such intimacy, of even touching his bed-sheets or fluffing his pillow, made Mallory color. "Perhaps a day nurse..." she ventured.

"Nothing like that to be found around these parts," Josie replied. "No, you'll have to do your best to take care of his needs."

Head still bent, Chase arched an eyebrow, his mouth twitching, as his silver gaze sought Mallory's.

Mallory felt her flush deepen, and a prickly heat inched beneath her arms and between her legs. Her clothes felt tight, constrictive.

"Don't worry, honey. An injury like this sort of gelds the stallion, if you get my meaning." She patted the torn end of the tape for the gauze binding firmly back into place on the roll.

Mallory's eyes widened. She certainly knew what *that* meant. Without meaning to, her eyes dropped to that par-ticular part of his anatomy.

Chase groaned, and the inside vee of his jeans twitched, as if he was checking to make sure all of his masculine parts were still intact.

Josie chuckled. "I imagine, with Chase, you'll have all

you can do to keep him down, keep him quiet. Hog-tie him to the bedpost if you have to.''

Though he didn't look at her, Chase's eyebrow inched suggestively higher. Mallory ignored him and stared at the paperwork Nurse Josie pushed under her nose.

''The doctor left a prescription that'll knock the spit and vinegar out of him for a few days. You can get it filled at the hospital pharmacy.''

''Thank you,'' she murmured.

''You take care, Chase,'' Josie continued, her hand resting on his forearm, ''and don't get them bandages wet. Spit baths only. Have Mallory here change it tomorrow, and for the next three days.'' Josie handed Mallory his shirt. ''He's all yours, honey. Now, you just have a world of fun with this old prickly pear, you hear? Just don't let him get the best of you.'' With that final bit of advice, Josie swept out of the examining room.

Mallory let the soft cotton western shirt slip through her fingers and slide onto her lap. Chase didn't look at her but fixed his gaze on the tangled shirt instead.

''Lewt's always…looked after me,'' he said, his voice strained. ''But don't imagine he'll…have much patience for…tuckin' me in. Or…buttonin' me up.''

Mallory slapped the bravest smile on her face that she could manage. Okay, she could do this. She could care for him in a perfectly professional, platonic way. ''I'll see to everything you need. It's my fault you're hurt, I know that. But when I'm done with you, you'll be good as new.''

Chase slowly lifted his eyes and stared at her.

Mallory stood. ''C'mon,'' she said, shaking out the shirt. ''Let's get you dressed.'' She held it open for him, but he could barely lift his arm, and when he tried, his features flattened with pain. Mallory eased the sleeve over his hand and his wrist, smoothing it up his arm and over his shoulder. She tried to avoid contact with his tanned, bare skin—but when she adjusted the collar at the back of his neck her fingertips grazed the short fine hairs of his nape and felt the warm, moist corded flesh.

She instinctively drew back—until she saw his eyelids lower. She hesitated, before she experimentally let her fingers wander beneath his collar and brazenly skip over the back of his neck. His eyelids drifted nearly closed and Mallory recognized an ache that had little to do with pain.

She was playing with fire; she knew it. She had no business testing the waters, because the spark that ran between them could affect her attempts to bring Peggy Sue home.

"It's going to be a trick to get your other arm in," she said softly.

"'Kay," he muttered through gritted teeth.

She guided his arm backward as best she could. He winced, and she eased the sleeve onto his hand and then his arm. "There."

He flexed, shouldering into the garment. Mallory automatically started working the pearl snaps. He took a deep breath and her fingertips accidentally grazed the wall of his bare muscled chest. Mallory set her mouth, forcing herself to appear unaffected.

She reached for the next snap, suddenly conscious that the shirt trailed onto the denim fly of his jeans. Her hand backtracked, as if it had a will of its own. Feeling foolish, she made a show of checking the snap she'd just fastened. "I, um, thought I missed one," she murmured.

"You didn't miss a thing," he said, a faint chuckle twisting his words.

Mallory refused to acknowledge the innuendo and fastened two more snaps, pausing at his belt buckle. "That should do it," she announced.

"For now."

Mallory warily glanced up at him, unable to detect what was hidden beneath that silver gaze. "You blame me, don't you?"

He snorted, then grimaced and clutched his ribs. "No. I blame myself. I should have had that horse put down."

"Chase—"

"She's too dangerous. I can't risk anyone else getting hurt."

"No one will. It was my fault. With a little time, a little attention—"

"Mallory. I can't take care of her anymore! Hell—" he drew a ragged breath "—I'm going to have to lean on you to get off this examining table."

"Don't worry about caring for Peggy Sue. Someone will—"

"No, they won't. Lewt's too old. Gabe's too inexperienced. And Tony? Forget it. He flat out refuses to get within twenty feet of her." He coughed, anchoring his elbow against his side. "Says she's the mustang with the evil eye."

"Oh, basche!"

Chase lifted an eyebrow. "Translation?"

Mallory looked surprised. She rarely slipped into the Narwhalian tongue. "Ridiculous," she said finally, gesturing with her hand, as if it were unimportant. "The animal will be gentled with time and a tender heart. She has a gift that perhaps few can see. Perhaps because they choose not to look."

"I have to put her down, Mallory. I'd rather cut my heart out than do it, but...I've given her enough time. I've—"

"You will cut out my heart if you destroy that horse, Chase," she implored, her hand settling on his arm. "You cannot."

His face contorted, indecision mixing with pain.

"Sell her to me! Let me be responsible."

"Forget it."

"Why? You've already said you don't want her, you can't handle her—"

Mallory's argument visibly wounded his cowboy pride, making him bristle. "I never said—" he sputtered "—I couldn't handle her."

"Of course not. I only meant…now…with your injuries." She paused. "There is only one option left. Me. I will stay and care for you…and for her. I will tame her, and in time you will be convinced to sell her to me."

"Never." Indicating the subject was closed, he attempted to straighten and slide off the table. Mallory quickly supported his elbow and let him lean into her. They swayed together for a moment, as one. Everything felt so right that she wanted to succumb to the closeness. It was Chase who pulled away. "The obvious reason…is she'll blight my reputation. She's one sick animal…and no one knows why. She comes from my stock. No matter who her daddy was, her mama was a champion."

"Perhaps it is her father's blood that has given her this gift."

He stared down at her, their faces but inches apart. Mallory could feel his breath on her cheek as his unflinching eyes bored into her. "Gift? What the hell is that supposed to mean?"

"I merely meant that she may be…special," Mallory said carefully. "Special, with traits few can recognize."

"Damn right, she's special. In ways I can't begin to explain. That's why I've never given up on her."

Her eyes never wavered from his. "Your loyalty will one day be rewarded," she predicted solemnly.

"What?"

"I have told you of the legend in my country, Chase.

About a horse with a unique and special power. One that brings goodness to those who recognize his needs, to those who make sacrifices to bring him aid and comfort. Perhaps if we do the same, to bring comfort to Peggy Sue—"

"You've *got* to be kidding me."

"No. It is true."

"What it is, Mallory, is all a bunch of hogwash. Some nice little tale, to keep all the peasants happy. I just got the tar knocked out of me by some crazy horse, and you're talking about legends and fairy tales? I thought I was the one with the concussion. But you…you need to get a grip and come back to the real world."

"I can tame the horse with the wild heart," she said emphatically, never backing down. "As for you, you have no choice but to give me the chance."

"You're telling me what? I have to do what?" he seethed raggedly, whirling and bumping her with his thigh. "You think I've no other choice?"

Mallory stood firm. "Because you want me to prove this thing to you."

Chase drew a long, rasping breath. Against his sides, his fingers clenched into white-knuckled fists. "Why?" he demanded. "Why do you think you can be the one to tame her?"

"I told you. Because it is written in the legend how the beast must be tamed. And I believe it. For my entire life I have sought to discover the legend's truth, and I have dedicated my life to—"

Chase rolled his eyes. "Oh, my—"

"No! You must trust me. Now there is more to the legend than you are ready to understand or accept. But someday you will. I promise you that, Chase."

Chapter Five

In the pickup, Chase sat between Mallory and Lewt and stared straight ahead. He was grateful Lewt didn't say much, but that was probably because it was nigh onto four in the morning. It was Mallory's steadfast determination, and the confident looks she exchanged with him, that wreaked havoc with his resolve. That, and the way her knee kept brushing against his every time they hit a pothole, the way her shoulder gently leaned into his every time Lewt took a corner. The physical distractions were driving him crazy...and sometimes they just plain hurt. Even with the painkiller.

Before they left the hospital Chase told her he'd think about letting her take care of the stupid horse. That was all. Nothing more, nothing less. Okay, so maybe he should let her have at it and find out for herself.

To make matters worse, he couldn't believe that she'd been babbling on about legends and all that goofy stuff. What a crock. It was incomprehensible that she actually believed any of it. He'd hardly known what to say to her.

Of course, the bottom line was that he should get rid of the damn horse. She was nothing but a menace. Why, she'd practically killed him last winter when she ran him down in the corral. He'd locked her up in the barn after that unfortunate incident, in a box stall that he kept repairing, thanks to her chewing and kicking and tantrum-throwing. Her rages were getting worse, and this time, when she'd kicked him, he'd honestly thought he was a goner.

He'd never had a horse he couldn't handle...and it grated on him no end, thinking how it had once been, with him and Skylar, and a horse called Peggy Sue. Things had been so different then....

Damn. If he didn't know better, he'd think the horse was grief-stricken. Like him. He vaguely wondered if they did counseling on four-year-old mares with an attitude.

Lewt pulled up to the back door and threw the truck in Park. Both he and Mallory climbed out. "You need help, Buster Brown?" he asked, using his pet name for Chase.

"Nah. I'm fine—just a little stiff. Be good as new in a coupla days."

Lewt squinted, his mouth puckering up as if he'd just sucked a lemon. "Yeah, sure, and that ain't what the doctor says."

"What do they know?" Chase blustered, hugging his arm close to his side. He scooched over on the seat to the passenger side and, with the toe of his boot, carefully reached for the ground. Mallory's hand slid beneath his elbow. Playing the tough guy, for Lewt's benefit, he considered shrugging her off—but looking into her angelic face, he couldn't bring himself to hurt her feelings. "Thanks," he said gruffly.

"Well, missy, better get the old fussbudget to bed," Lewt advised, reaching in his vest pocket. "Here's them pills what the doc ordered." He extended them to her.

"Reckon he should throw one back afore he goes plumb out of his head with pain."

"I'm fine," Chase ground out.

Lewt snorted. "Ain't nuthin' worse than a broke rib," he announced. "Nothin'."

"Yeah, and I'm not out here in the middle of the night looking for sympathy," Chase retorted.

"Good. 'Cause you ain't gettin' any," Lewt said agreeably. "Be seein' you young'uns in the morning." He thumped the flat of his hand against his belly. "Sleep tight, ya hear?" Chuckling, he sauntered off into dark toward the bunkhouse.

"I don't know why I keep him around," Chase muttered, painfully negotiating the back steps.

"Probably because he's just so lovable." She held the screen door open for Chase, then pushed open the back door.

"Huh. There's nothing lovable around here, Mallory. We're all just a bunch of used-up, down-on-our-luck cowboys." He walked past her and into the kitchen. "Keep that in mind. Because I'm warnin' you."

Mallory followed, letting the screen door slam. Putting down her purse, she went to the sink, got a glass of water and extended it to him. He took it while she worked the top off the prescription bottle. "One before bed," she reminded. "It'll probably help you sleep most of the morning away."

"Can't afford to," he grumbled. "I got chores."

"No, *I've* got chores," she emphasized calmly, offering him the painkiller on her open palm. "I know the routine. I can manage breakfast, and graining the horses, and Peggy Sue, and whatever else needs to be done."

Chase tossed the pill back and took a long pull on the water. "You worked that in pretty nice. About Peggy Sue."

"I can handle her, Chase."

He intentionally let a second slip away. Mostly because he wanted to control his reaction—but partially because he needed to beat back the memories. She was so different from Sharon. His ex-wife would have flounced off and said she wasn't going to be bothered by any dirty horses. She would have yapped at him for not being nice just because *he* was feeling miserable. "Tell me. Why do you think you can handle her?" he asked. "Oh, I know. It was the legend. You looked in a mirror, and it said you were the fairest equestrienne of them all, is that it?"

"That," she said succinctly, her mouth lifting an irresistible fraction of an inch at the corner, "is a fairy tale."

"Yes, well, if the shoe fits…"

"Aha! Another fairy tale," she chided.

"Mallory—"

"You are not ready to believe! If I tell you…" She shook her head, her blond hair swirling over her shoulders. "No, you will still not believe. I see it in your eyes."

He sought her out, intentionally fastening her, holding her, with a dark gaze. "Just tell me," he said grudgingly. "Get this over with, so I can go to bed."

She lowered her lashes demurely, unaware the overhead kitchen light illuminated the faint flush of color in her cheeks. There was an innocence about her Chase couldn't identify, but it tugged at him, making him want to tell her it was okay, that she could tell him anything. That at least he'd listen, even if he didn't believe her.

"I didn't tell you the truth," she said slowly. "Not all of it. The horse—the one in the legend—is not a horse at all, but a…a *unicorn.*" She breathed the word, her voice lifting with wonder.

He rolled his eyes, vaguely wondering if the medication

was making him hear things. *A unicorn?* She said the horse was a *unicorn?*

"You said you wanted to know!" Mallory's voice lifted petulantly. And she was, Chase conceded, not a petulant person.

He heaved a sigh. "Okay. I do."

"The name of my country, Narwhal, means 'unicorn of the sea.'" She paused. "Historically, it is said that when the world was young, the unicorn were banished to Narwhal because they were different. The unicorn, you know, loves freedom. It also loves that which is pure and innocent."

He stared at her. "Wait a minute. This is pretend picture-book stuff. You know that, don't you, Mallory?"

She looked away and could not meet his eyes. An uncomfortable feeling scuttled down Chase's spine. What was he dealing with? A nut? One who had some crazy belief in unicorns and fairies?

"It is said," she continued, a slight quaver to her voice, "that the estate where my family now lives is where the unicorn once thrived. They ran in the meadow. They—" she cleared her throat uncomfortably "—multiplied there. And it is said they danced on the waters."

Chase couldn't help it; he raised a disbelieving brow.

"However, these were special animals, Chase. Legend has it…that they could only be tamed by a chaste and innocent maid."

Chase's brow inched higher.

"I believe," Mallory said, "it is this innocence that Peggy Sue trusts."

Chase's brow dropped back into place; his jaw slid off center.

"A sense, perhaps. Unwitting, but—"

"What're you saying?"

"You saw her with me. You saw how calm she was. How trusting."

"It was your voice. Your instincts," he argued.

"No. *Her* instincts. I think that Peggy Sue trusts me, because I've never—" her smile tightened, hovering between apologetic and embarrassed "—been with a man. Not…in that way."

He stared at her, and her gaze faltered.

Chase didn't hear the rest of her explanation. Something akin to a red-hot poker, finished him off in the chest, then it seared his groin. Hell, he couldn't even breathe, and here he was thinking of sex—and Mallory's nubile, untouched curves. And a vision of a dagnabbed unicorn running around on his place shot through his brain.

"I suppose *virgin* sounds old-fashioned, especially in this day and age. But I—"

"You're a virgin," he said flatly. "Untasted, untouched, untempted."

Her hand fluttered to his sleeve. "Oh, no. Not untempted, Chase," she said, an innocent lilt lacing her voice. "Never that. Just unwilling to give in to what doesn't feel right and lasting."

Chase's eyelids winched closed. One thought burned a crater into what little gray matter he was nursing back to health: *he wished to hell that pain pill would kick in.* He wished it with his whole beat-up, broken-down heart. He needed it now more than ever.

The clock over the kitchen stove hummed, the refrigerator kicked in and the window, still open over the sink, let in a cooling gust of wind. Everything was the same…but different. One more revelation to add to the mix. One more complication.

Mallory couldn't be just a fly-by-night heiress who liked a good romp in the hay, a few laughs and a cold beer. Oh, no. That would be too easy. She had to be the paragon of virtue. She had to be an out-and-out greenhorn when it came to all this flirting they'd been doing. And she'd had absolutely no idea where it was headed...or at least where Chase had hoped it was headed.

Key word: *hoped.*

Because it sure as hell wasn't heading there anymore. No way. It was heading to be shelved. Right up there with all this hocus-pocus stuff, about unicorns living in her meadow and how she, as the fairest maiden of them all, could tame them and because of her virtuous behavior. It was all a bunch of malarky.

He felt like he'd been duped. In more ways than one.

Damnation, and here he'd been thinking about letting her sleep in the big bed—with him—before she went back to Narwhal.

"Chase?" Mallory gently prodded him, her fingers tightening on his sleeve.

"Yeah?"

"You've lost a little color. Perhaps it was the pill...?"

"No. I'm fine. I—I'm just not used to finding out those kinds of...intimate things...about my houseguests." He looked at her. Really looked. But she didn't retract one word. "I just assumed that...when you kissed me—out there, in the barn—that maybe we'd take up where we left off. Someday."

She didn't say anything. Just gazed at him, with baby-blue eyes that were to die for, with a smile that he had touched and tasted with his tongue. With a halo of fine blond hair that only hours ago had tickled his temple and caught in his five o'clock shadow.

"Well, hell, you did kiss me, didn't you?" he demanded irritably, pulling away from her touch. "Or was I hallucinating the whole thing?"

"I...yes...I kissed you."

Drat it all! How could the woman offer up an enticing smile and make such an admission at the same time?

"You asked me to," she explained. "To make it better."

"Yeah. Well...under the circumstances—" He broke off, trying to imagine how a woman so innately seductive could not have firsthand knowledge of the birds and the bees. Something did not equate. "If I'd known I wouldn't have asked you to...break some personal code or something. I wouldn't have messed around with someone inexperienced and—" *Crazy?*

She laughed, a tinkling little sound that burrowed right in under his heart. "I wouldn't have done it if I didn't want to, Chase."

"Yeah. Well, you sure fooled me. It was a pretty experienced kiss."

"You thought so?" She looked inordinately pleased. "Sometimes things feel right, I suppose. Like they're meant to be." Before he could protest, she said, "Like how things were meant to be with Peggy Sue and me, I suppose."

"Mallory..."

"Chase, give me this opportunity. What will it hurt? You can see for yourself if the legend is true. Now that you know—" her voice changed, dropping ever so subtly to a whisper "—*everything* about me."

"And it's somethin' I could have got along fine without knowing, thank you very much," he groused.

"Did I embarrass you?" she said in concern. "That was not my intention. I only needed to tell you because of Peggy Sue...because I want to help you. And I see something in her I think I can help."

"This is the craziest damn thing I've ever heard in my life. You honestly think that—one virgin to another—you can relate?"

Mallory's eyelashes coquettishly swept her cheek; he willed himself not to react. "Something like that, Chase."

"That horse is nothing but a half-wit. A wild mustang without a lick of sense. That's all."

"That is what you believe now, but you may change your mind."

"Highly unlikely."

Disappointment etched her features. He guessed Mallory imagined he would forbid her to work with Peggy Sue. What then? He knew she'd stay long enough to see him back on his feet, but after that there'd be no reason to stay.

The woman was pleasant enough to have around, he allowed. If she could do something with that nutty horse, why should he care? "You really want to do this?" he asked.

"I need to do this, Chase. For her. And for me."

"Tell me. You don't really think she's a unicorn, do you?"

Mallory gnawed her lower lip, her brow furrowing indecisively. "Don't be silly," she said finally. "The horse has traits similar to those referred to in the legend, that's all. She couldn't possibly be a real unicorn. How many people would believe that?"

Okay, so maybe she wasn't totally out of it. He shrugged and made a snap decision, oblivious to the pain it caused him. "Okay, then. Do it." When she looked up at him, her face was wreathed in smiles…and, damn it all, if she didn't look just like an angel.

"Thank you, thank you," she whispered.

He started to nod, but she stopped him short. She lifted to the tips of her toes and carefully planted a warm, affectionate kiss on his cheek. Looping his arm around her, he impulsively pulled her tight against his ribs, refusing to give in to the pain. "No, babycakes, like this," he said huskily, turning his head to the side and catching her mouth. In one split second, he lost himself to the ecstasy of one mind-bending kiss.

Just like before, he thought numbly, loosening his grasp. *Just like before.*

When he reluctantly pulled back, he stared straight down into Mallory's wide-eyed look of surprise.

"We were so close...I could have hurt you," she said softly, imperceptibly pulling back and letting her hand trail over the dressings on his torso.

"Yeah," he said grimly. "You just could have."

"But—"

"Maybe you already did." He looked down at the woman in his arms and felt himself tumbling into an abyss of want and desire—and knew it could never happen. Not with her. Not with Miss Chaste Mallory Chevalle of Narwhal. "And you remember, if that horse hurts one hair on your head," he warned, "it's history. I mean it. I'll put her down. I swear I will."

Chapter Six

Mallory hadn't slept. She kept thinking about everything Chase had said. She kept thinking about Peggy Sue. She was on the verge of something big, and the knowledge of that left her giddy with relief and anticipation.

Perhaps, her prayers to find the elusive Cornelle bloodlines had been answered.

She thought of her father, and a sense of longing filled her. She ached to see him, to comfort him and assure him all would be well. She was certain that the discovery of this ''demon'' horse would strengthen him and give him a sense of purpose. She imagined her father overcome with joy, she envisioned him leading the animal with the Cornelle blood to the meadow and setting her free. His dreams would be realized, his desire to restore peace to Narwhal's meadow would be met. She knew it would happen, she just knew it.

Soon, she repeated silently, sending the message a world away, across the ocean, *soon all will be well. And you have Chase Wells to thank,* she added, *because he did not give up on an impossible, strong-willed mare, one who only wants to come home.*

As the first light of dawn crept into her room, Mallory gratefully tossed back the covers and dressed. She sat on the unmade bed and pulled on her boots. Unexpectedly, a chill coursed through her and she shivered uncontrollably.

This was the first day she would spend alone caring for Peggy Sue. The magnitude of what she was doing and what she knew was overwhelming. She could not afford to fail. No matter what, she had to see this through, and she had to make it work. Peggy Sue, who was everything in the plan, was not really a consideration. It was her nature to respond—and respond she would. Mallory would see to it.

The three cowboys, each independent, each as different as the next, would prove small obstacles, nothing more. They might be skittish around the horse, but she would earn their respect. The American term was *spunky*. Yes. They would call her spunky.

It was Chase who stymied her. Chase—irascible and stubborn, who would eye her progress and challenge it. Mallory may have connected with Peggy Sue on an instinctual level, but there was a connection between Chase and Peggy Sue that she could not identify. It bothered her, and she sensed it could cripple her purpose.

Chase was the key. He was the one who would say "yea" or "nay."

Even so, he could be won over, she assured herself. A time would come when she would ask to take Peggy Sue back to Narwhal…and she could not give him any choice but to agree that it would be best.

It was early morning quiet when Mallory slipped into Peggy Sue's stall. The horse eyed her suspiciously, her ears flicking back.

"I told you, it will be okay," Mallory soothed. "But you have to know you hurt him. You hurt him really bad." She intentionally turned her back and dumped a scoop of oats into the feed bucket. She was wary—until she felt the horse inquisitively nuzzle her shoulder. "No, nothing has changed. I went to the hospital with him last night, that was all."

Peggy Sue whickered quietly.

"No, he's not a bad man. Chase Wells is just…a man." The description, as well as the implications, hung heavily in the back of Mallory's mind. She thought of Chase sitting hunched, shirtless, on the examining table. So strong, so maddeningly sensible…so take-your-breath-away sexy.

Peggy Sue nudged her sternly.

Mallory immediately straightened, a flash of guilt reminding her that Chase Wells was off limits. "Yes, well, I'll be taking care of you for a while, whether you like it or not. I've gotten you a reprieve, but you are going to have to cooperate." Mallory turned, extending the back of her hand for Peggy Sue to smell. The horse's nostrils flared, then she threw her great head. "You don't scare me. I know you, and I know what you want. You can trust me, Peggy Sue. I'll never betray you. I'll do what's best for you…and for my father…and for Narwhal. But you have to let me."

Peggy Sue snorted and turned her head disdainfully away from the feed bucket.

"Yes, and you may feel that way now, but consider it. There are things we have to do. Like get you out of this dreary stall. We have to get out in the corral, in the sunshine. We have to run in the pasture and go down by the creek." Peggy Sue blinked, her long, dark lashes swiping in surprise at her cheek. "We can do it," Mallory continued. "But only together. That will be the only way. Chase said."

Sidestepping, Peggy Sue inched closer to the feed bucket, surreptitiously peering over the edge.

"Okay, so I added a little honey. Someone—I think it was Chase—mentioned that you liked it. I'll admit it, I'm not above bribery." Ever so slightly, Peggy Sue's nose quivered. Mallory reached into her back pocket. "I brought the currycomb, too. So I could brush you while you eat."

Peggy Sue swung her head around to give her a flat stare.

"Hey, if you don't want to—" Mallory shrugged and started backing from the stall. Just as quickly, Peggy Sue harrumphed in resignation and dipped her nose into the feed bucket. Mallory bit back a smile and automatically brushed the horse's neck.

They stood there for a long time, while Peggy Sue contentedly chewed her oats and slurped her honey. Mallory comfortably stroked long paths down the horse's neck and withers. Peggy Sue's coat was shaggy and unkempt, her steel-gray coloring dingy, resembling the hue of a soiled dishcloth.

"I have four horses at home," Mallory said idly, continuing to stroke Peggy Sue's back, her belly, "and I spoil them terribly. The stable is next to our meadow. Like the land where you used to run in the West, I suppose. With thousands and thousands of acres." Mallory stopped, reminiscing over the home she loved, when she noticed a perceptible pause in Peggy Sue's chewing. "There are springs that bubble right up from the ground." She razed the currycomb over Peggy Sue's rump.

Peggy Sue lifted her head, ever so slightly, from the feed bucket.

"Did you ever run through a spring like that, Peggy Sue?" Mallory asked dreamily. "With the water splashing beneath your hooves and spattering your backside?"

Peggy Sue stood stock still.

"Maybe with Chase?" she asked.

Snorting, Peggy Sue shook her great hide, stamped, then shifted her attention back to the feed bucket.

"Well, it was just a question. You don't have to get so irritable." Mallory continued to brush the dirt and dust from Peggy Sue's back. "I miss my home. I used to go riding every morning, before anyone else in the house was up."

Behind her, the gate to the stall rattled, and Mallory looked over her shoulder to find Lewt standing behind it, his elbow propped on the top rail. "Chase know you're in here?"

"We agreed I'd take care of Peggy Sue for a while. She seems to trust me," Mallory said, avoiding his perceptive gaze.

He thoughtfully rearranged the wad of tobacco in his cheek. "This his last-ditch effort, huh?"

"Excuse me?" American colloquialisms were so confusing.

"This horse ain't nuthin' but a trial," he said. "Few years back, Chase claimed she'd bring him something special—and fool that I was, I believed him."

"You don't think she's special?"

"Missy, this horse ain't brought him nuthin' but trouble." He shook his head, spitting into the dust at his feet. "She turned on him, at one of the lowest times in his life."

"Horses sense things."

"Mebbe. But I can't figure her out, and it ain't for lack of tryin'. It's like she wants to hurt and keep on hurtin', till it's all used up inside her."

Mallory filed the information away and concentrated on her grooming. "My father used to say wild horses are unpredictable. They lash out."

"Yeah, and you better take care to watch yourself,

missy. With this horse. And with Chase, too, I reckon. It's the one thing they have in common, lashing out. Even when they don't mean to."

Mallory found everything she needed in the kitchen and tried not to make too much noise finding it. She liked to think pancakes were a comfort food. They were, after all, warm and sweet and filling. Chase could use a dose of comfort now. She was sure of it.

When the tray was ready, she put a hunk of butter in the center of the stacked pancakes and a creamer of warmed syrup on the side. She supposed Chase wouldn't appreciate it, but she added a single wildflower she'd plucked out by the horse tank. It looked a little too delicate for his raw strength, a little too soft for his rough edges...but she'd make a joke of it and give it to him, anyway.

Carefully, silently, she carried the tray up the steps and into the second-floor hallway. She was about to bump open the door to his room, which was already cracked, when Lewt's voice stopped her.

"What're you gonna do, give her enough rope to hang herself, that it?"

"I told you..." Chase coughed, then groaned. "She wants to spend some time with the horse, that's all."

"Plumb crazy, if you ask me."

"What's it going to hurt?"

"Hurt?" Lewt exploded. "Lookee there, who's layin' in bed. I'd guess I'd call that hurtin'."

"I don't want anything to happen to her, either. But she's so...determined."

Lewt muttered.

"You said yourself, she knows her horses."

"Yeah, well, she don't know that one."

"I—"

Mallory refused to hear any more. She lifted her hand, poised it and gently rapped on the open door with her knuckles. Then she opened the door and walked in. Chase, instead of being propped up in the bed as she expected, sat on the edge of it.

In his white cotton underwear. And with a twelve-inch gauze dressing around his middle. That, and nothing else.

Mallory swallowed and looked away. From her peripheral vision, she saw Chase quickly pull the sheet across his lap.

Lewt chuckled. "Watch it. You're movin' pretty fast there, buster. Gonna break another one of them ribs."

Trying to appear unaffected, Mallory took a deep breath and placed the tray on the dresser. "I thought you'd like some breakfast," she said. "And coffee."

"Thanks...but I could have come down."

"Ain't you got one of them robes, or smokin' jackets or somethin'?" Lewt prodded, motioning to his closet. "Hate to embarrass the missy here, seein' you in your skivvies."

Chase glared at him, his knuckles going white as he clutched the sheet tighter against his groin.

"It's all right," Mallory said, ignoring the heat crawling up her neck. "I wanted to check Chase's bandages, anyway. See that everything is still tight."

Lewt's weathered face screwed up, as if he was trying not to laugh. "Well, best let you folks get on to your doctorin'." Without waiting for their reply, he went out in the hall and shut the door after him. Once there, he guffawed. Loudly.

Chase's eyes drifted closed. "And you still think he's lovable?" he asked.

"Oh—" she shrugged, dismissing it "—he doesn't mean any harm. He cares about you."

"He needs to mind his own business. Now he's worried about you taking care of Peggy Sue."

"I heard."

"That's all?"

"We had a good morning. Peggy Sue and I came to an understanding." The look he shot her made her revise the statement. "Of course it helped that you told me she likes a little honey in her feed. I got on her good side with that."

He lifted his shoulder, then winced.

The action seemed to hurt her, too. As if she could feel every pinprick of Chase's pain. She wished she could go to him, to offer him comfort. But she needed to keep her dealings with him on a purely professional level. That would be the only way they could last...because her yearnings were becoming too hard to veil. It was as if she needed him to make herself whole. It was a feeling she'd never before experienced. And she couldn't experience it now...not when she was so close to knowing about the unicorn—or the Cornelles.

"You should eat," she said softly, changing the subject. "Would you like me to bring you a chair? Or would you rather lie back? I can fix your pillows, with the tray, and..." She caught his smoldering gaze and trailed off.

An uncontested second of awareness slipped away.

"Bring me the tray," he said finally. "And sit beside me."

A flicker of apprehension skitted through her. "On the bed?"

"Mmm-hmm." He tucked the sheet under his thigh.

Mallory did as he asked. For the life of her she didn't know why. It was confusing, all of it. She helped him steady the tray on his lap, then settled onto the mattress beside him, intentionally putting a good inch of Wyoming air between them.

Chase grinned and eyed the button-shaped wildflower, then the coffee cup. He said nothing about the flower. "You make good coffee?"

"Probably not. I prefer tea."

"Ah. All that fancy upbringing."

This time, Mallory was not offended.

Chase hooked a finger beneath the handle and lifted the cup. Leaning over, he blew across the steaming surface, then curved his lips against the rim. His eyes narrowed as he took the first swallow. "Not bad," he allowed, carefully setting the cup back on the tray.

With that little bit of praise, Mallory felt her heart swell. "The pancakes are better," she said. "And you need something solid and warm in your stomach."

He plunged his fork into the stack and stabbed a small bite before dipping it into the pitcher of syrup. "I know, I know," he said affably, before slipping the forkful into his mouth. "It's been said I have no manners."

"I don't care."

He regarded her, chewing thoughtfully. "You don't, do you? You care about the most unusual things." His brow furrowed. "Huh. Pretty good pancakes, actually."

Mallory thought she must be glowing from the inside out.

"Tell me about your dad," he said. "Is he into all this legends and stuff?"

"My father? Oh, he is well versed in the legends of Narwhal, and he saw to it that understanding the legends should be part of my education. They have historical value. And there are lessons to be learned."

Chase poured a generous amount of syrup over the rest of the pancakes. "I see. Sort of like, 'And the moral of this story is...'"

"Excuse me?"

He waved the fork, explaining, "It's an American thing. A joke. To putting the lesson of the story into something funny."

She stared at him. "I don't think there is anything funny about the legend."

"No, I...I meant..." He broke off and stuck a sizable bite into his mouth, considering. "Wait a minute. You've got to admit there is something funny about a young woman who drives all the way out to Wyoming by herself to find this special horse for her father, and having her make me think that she thinks it could be a unicorn. I mean, last night you almost convinced me you were serious about this."

Mallory blinked. "I am serious about this. About...finding the horse, I mean."

"But the unicorn part, that's funny, isn't it?" A moment of silence filled the room. "Or...is it my concussion?"

"I think it is the concussion. We all say things when we are out of our head."

He chewed thoughtfully, then pushed the tray back onto his knees and away from his torso. "You gonna check my bandages?"

Concern furrowed her brow. "Yes. Are they bothering you?"

"Yeah. A lot." He lifted his arm to let her see where the gauze had pulled away, leaving red, raised marks.

"Oh, Chase—" her fingertips skimmed the red swelling "—I'm so sorry."

"I am, too, honey."

At the endearment, her gaze slid apprehensively over to his and her touch imperceptibly pulled free. "Maybe I could redo it, but I have to put a new gauze pad on it later tonight."

"Could you rub it? I can't reach it and it's driving me crazy."

Mallory hesitated, her fingers still hovering near his side. "Won't that make it worse?"

"Nah."

"Well, I don't know…" She pulled back indecisively.

"Mallory," he reminded gently, "you said you'd care for me."

"Of course. I did." She lifted the tray from his lap and put it back on the dresser. "The nurse did give me some cream, but I didn't think you'd need it yet." She reached into the pocket of her jeans and pulled out a small complimentary tube. Then she sat back beside him, swiveling her hips away from his. Dabbing a small amount of cream on her fingertips, she laved it on the inflamed skin.

"It's warm," he whispered. "From being in your jeans."

She dipped her head lower and concentrated on another spot, nearer his chest. Time evaporated as she worked it in.

"Does that embarrass you," he asked, "how your body makes mine warm?"

His suggestion made her quiver. Her chest vibrated, her thighs trembled. The only way to repulse the feelings, she decided, would be a businesslike demeanor. "I don't think patients say that to their nurses," she reproved, moving to the cup-shaped indentation below his pecs.

"Maybe not, but…mmm…you've got good hands."

"Chase," she chided. "You shouldn't say things like that. Now I know you are joking."

He chuckled. "But, honey," he protested, "I can say anything I want. No matter how crazy it sounds. Because this concussion is making me talk out of my head, remember? And right now, I'll admit I'm about out of my head with wanting you. And I've been lying here all morning just wondering what I'm going to have to do to get you to meet me halfway.''

Chapter Seven

Mallory slapped the cap back on the ointment, and concentrated on getting the top screwed on. Saying nothing she rose from the bed and put the tube on the nightstand next to his bed.

"Mallory?"

"I tried to tell you. I don't take these things lightly." She lifted the tray to carry it down to the kitchen. "I'm working with Peggy Sue this afternoon, and I'll check on you later." She turned her back and took two steps.

"Wait."

She should have kept on walking, but something, perhaps it was the tone in his voice—conciliatory?—that made her hesitate.

"I need something off that tray."

She glanced down in confusion. He'd cleaned the plate and finished the last drop of coffee. Still, she turned back, offering it to him.

He reached, avoiding the dirty dishes, to pluck the fragile blue wildflower from the top of the tray. "I don't take these things lightly, either," he said, studying the flower as he twirled it between thumb and forefinger. "They kind of soften up old, crusty hearts. Like the one I've got."

"Chase, I—"

"Put the tray down and talk to me," he said softly. "It's been a long, lonely morning, thinking of you out there in that barn, wishing I could be with you, to see what's going on. With you and Peggy Sue."

His reference to the horse put a dent in her resolve. No matter what, she had to put the welfare of that animal first. She put the tray aside and faced him. To her surprise, he extended the flower.

"For you," he said. The gesture took her breath away. "You've got the strength and resiliency of a wildflower," he added, gently waggling the slender stem, "yet you're just as fragile. Of course, sometimes I think you're as thorny as a rose."

Mallory accepted it, then absently traced a petal with the tip of one ovaled nail and chuckled. "When I was twenty-one, a suitor sent me a room full of roses," she confided softly, "but this? This means more."

"Why?"

"Because I suspect it is genuinely given."

"It is."

She couldn't meet his eyes; her focus remained fixed on the delicate petals.

He put his hand out, palm side up, as if he expected her to place hers into it. "Talk to me a minute. There are things we need to discuss."

Her hand, as if it had a will of its own, inched over to his. His palm was thick and callused, and she laid hers upon it. His fingers curled warmly, possessively, around hers, and he drew her to his side.

Without thinking, she sat back down beside him.

"I am a rather...*experienced*...man," he said finally. "I know you know what that means. And what you told me last night changes things. I don't go about...*deflowering*," he emphasized, "innocent young things. It goes against my nature to take something that precious away."

Her gaze remained riveted on the single, long-stemmed flower. "I shouldn't have told you," she said finally, her voice barely above a whisper. "Now you'll treat me like a child."

His hand tightened around hers. "No. I'm glad you did."

Her gaze, hopeful and tentative, collided with his—and neither could tear away from the binding force that held them.

The air in her lungs barely stirred, making her light-headed and weak.

A pulsing need throbbed through his veins, making him sizzle with want.

"It must sound crazy to you, to hear that I'm twenty-five years old, and I've chosen to keep myself for the one man, the right man," she said finally. "But I don't want a string of broken affairs and meaningless relationships. I want the kind of commitment that lasts forever. I believe in that."

He snorted as if something she said amused him. "'Forever' men are pretty hard to find these days."

"Perhaps."

"You kissed me. Two times yesterday."

"I shouldn't have."

"Maybe not. Because I'm not a 'forever' kind of man, Mallory." His warning made torment roll through her blue eyes, but he wouldn't allow her to pull away. "That kind of intimacy tempted me, honey. With all the things I said I'd never have. I'm a cowboy you can't tie down. But I've thought a lot about it this morning. And how I feel about you, and what you've brought out here to the Bar C.''

She lifted her shoulders. ''What have I brought you, but trouble? You remind me I am an inconvenience.''

A chuckle rumbled through his broad chest, making him wince. He coughed over his discomfort. ''You are. And I hate to admit it, but I love it.''

The corners of her mouth lifted in a half smile.

''I like your energy, honey, and I like your smile. And I like—'' his gaze slipped down, over her rump, to the mattress and rumpled sheets they sat on, ''—thinking of you in my bed.'' Chase heard the short intake of air, but Mallory's features never creased with denial or insult. ''But it's not going to happen,'' he added, ''because I found out along the way that I'm not the sticking kind of man.''

''What are you saying?''

''That we'll both be a whole lot better off if you take your best shot with Peggy Sue, find out she isn't what you think she is, and then be on your way.''

''You want me to go home.''

''We're both leaning toward each other, Mallory. Can't you feel it?'' He drew her hand to his thrumming bare chest. ''It's right here. Right in the heart. And it's not any good, not for either of us. You certainly gave me a number-one reason last night.''

Against his taut flesh, Mallory's hand stiffened. ''Well, certainly I can feel something for you, without—without acting on my emotions, or—''

Chase squeezed her hand, silencing her. ''Can you?'' he asked, his voice provocatively low, husky. ''I feel you tremble, honey, and it ain't because you're scared. It's because you want me…about as much as I want you. Neither one of us wants broken promises doggin' our steps, so let's just forget about it and move on from here.''

A week had passed since that fateful encounter. It had shaken Mallory to the core—suddenly she knew the depth and breadth of a man's emotions. She had felt the strength in the firm hold he kept upon her, she had experienced the rhythm of life reverberating through his body.

She had never felt so close to another man, except for her father, ever before. And this was different. Entirely different.

Chase made her feel treasured and unique; he brought her confidence and composure. He spoke to her softly and with respect, yet honestly and—sometimes—with raw emotion. She could hear it in his voice and it made her quiver, from the inside out.

The way he looked at her, through his slitted, suggestive silver gaze, made her feel wanton and wild. Even reckless. As if her body were daring her, taunting her, to take risks and find fulfillment.

She ached to laugh with him and to tease.

But she couldn't. Because she knew very well where it would lead.

To his warm, waiting mouth and the safety of his arms…and he'd warned her of the outcome of that. So all she had left were the memories that she had emblazoned into her brain, to carry with her when she left this place. This remote, remarkable place, where Chase Wells thrived. It was rugged country, but it suited him.

She wondered, vaguely, how he'd do in Narwhal. There were similarities, to be sure. The space of her family's estate mimicked his ranch. The mountains that drew your eyes to the distance, the fecund scent of earth and air that made you breathe deep.

She would like to take him to her family's stables. To see him wearing jeans, instead of jodhpurs, as he saddled up a horse. Cowboy boots instead of riding boots. A dove-gray cowboy hat instead of a black riding helmet.

The stable boys would find him amusing, but they would respect his differences. For he was a man who earned respect. He had already proved that he was fair and kind and honest.

Last night, she realized he was nearly out of clean shirts and had done a load of laundry. It had been a strange, intimate experience to wash a man's clothes. The scent of them! A curious mixture of leather and the horehound candy he favored and kept in a tin in his breast pocket.

She'd run her fingers over the frayed cuff, where the sharp edge of his watch had worn away the fold. She'd finger-pressed the nubby texture inside the collar, where the stubble of his beard chafed. She'd noted the thin, worn fabric on the elbows of his long-sleeved shirts and the tear on the shoulder he claimed occurred when Peggy Sue head-butted him into a nail protruding from the box stall. Strange. Knowing that the shirts had been next to his skin made her handle them with something similar to reverence.

Later, propped with pillows in an easy chair, he had read the stock report, while she had made a clumsy attempt to repair the damage with a needle and thread. He'd told her to forget it, but she couldn't…it was as if she were compelled to fix that one small thing for him.

But it was more than that. It was the memory of sharing the same cozy room, after dusk, when the uncovered windows were black with shadows. The way he tipped the lampshade his direction, sending a shaft of light over the thick hump of his shoulder. The way he'd pulled the paper down to gaze over the top edge at her, and said she was going to make somebody a fine wife someday, what with all her Suzy Homemaker activities.

Mallory had no idea who this Suzy Homemaker person

was…but she liked the sound of it. So she just laughed and
tried harder to make her stitches more even, more perfect.

More than once in the last week he'd grin at her sheep-
ishly and handed her the coffeepot, saying she'd missed her
calling with the tea. She indulged him and took pleasure in
doing so.

So many precious, priceless memories she'd accumu-
lated—and in such a short time. It was going to tear her
heart out when she had to leave.

But her father needed her, and every day she was away
from him was a day she had lost for the both of them.

The progress she had made with Peggy Sue was remarkable, but Chase had no idea how far she had come. He still
wasn't able to move around like he used to, and though
he'd made a few trips to the barn and grudgingly admitted
Peggy Sue looked better, he had no idea how smart the
horse was, or how capable. Mallory was half afraid when
he found out, he'd never part with her.

The cowboys maintained a respectable distance, but they
were curious about all the work she was doing with Peggy
Sue, no doubt about that. When she managed to ease a
halter over Peggy Sue's head, they were confounded. That
horse, they muttered, had never let anyone near her ears or
her fetlock, not without a down-and-dirty fight. The vet,
they claimed, had had to knock her out when he checked
that goofy-looking knot on her forehead.

When she snapped a lead on and coaxed the horse to
walk out into the alleyway of the barn, Gabe unexpectedly
walked in on her and went chalk white, his color fading
like that of a cartoon character's. "Does Chase know
you're doin' this?" he demanded, his voice shaky as he
backpedaled nearer the door.

Peggy Sue planted all four hooves and fixed him with a
cold, hard stare.

Mallory tugged on the lead; Peggy Sue refused to budge. "He knows," she said.

Gabe's eyes rolled. "I don't think he figured you'd be takin' her out of the stall."

"How am I to train her if I don't?"

Peggy Sue pawed the ground. Once. Twice. Her hoof struck with deadly force, with warning.

"Ma'am, I..." Gabe inclined his head, tipping it in deference to the skittish animal.

Mallory tightened her hold on the lead, but her voice went soft, calming. "Peggy Sue, hush.... We have promises between us. But it is a long road home to them. You have to remember that." Peggy Sue's hoof struck again. This time with resignation.

"Ma'am, you're pushin' your luck. And Chase warned me that if anything happened to you, with her—"

"Gabe, we're fine," Mallory protested. "Peggy Sue knows it can't be just her and me. Not forever. She knows that other people are going to be here, watching, seeing her progress." Mallory whisked an affectionate hand over the horse's muzzle. "Right, baby?"

Gabe winced. "Ma'am, she's gonna bite you, you do that again."

Mallory laughed. Even Peggy Sue looked over at him, amused. "She's too smart for that. She'd never bite the hand that feeds her. Right, baby?" Mallory crooned, chucking her under the chin. Peggy Sue's whicker was like an endorsement. "I just thought I'd bring her out in the alley to groom her for a minute. It will be a change of scenery for both of us. That's all."

Gabe said nothing and rocked back on his heels to watch. With the lead in one hand, Mallory used her other to stroke the currycomb down Peggy Sue's gaunt sides.

"She's gainin' some weight," Gabe allowed.

"A little."

Mallory kept brushing but felt the lead tense in her other hand. Glancing over at Peggy Sue, she saw her nostrils flare and her eyes flash. Mallory automatically tightened her hold as Peggy Sue threw her head and knocked Mallory backward. She stumbled but kept her feet, even as she turned to see Chase silhouetted in the doorway.

"What the devil's goin' on?" he roared. "You got that animal out of the stall?"

Peggy Sue reared, ripping the lead from Mallory's hand, and then—there were no two ways about it—all hell broke loose.

The three of them—Mallory, Chase, and Gabe—stood outside the sliding door of the barn and watched Peggy Sue run past the corral and through the open gate out into the pasture. The lead rope trailed behind her, the end skipping over the ground at her heels.

The muscle along Chase's jaw twitched uncontrollably, and he held his arm tightly against his ribs. Peggy Sue had practically run him over in her flight to get out of the barn.

"Chase? Are you all right?" Mallory asked, her hand sliding above his elbow.

"Hell, yes, I'm okay. It's that blasted horse that—"

"Well, you scared her! What do you expect?" Mallory retorted. "You can't come blustering in, and—"

"Blustering? I wasn't blustering," he muttered, folding both arms across his middle and grimacing.

"You *were* blustering," she said firmly. "Just like my father, when he worries about things he shouldn't."

"The only thing I was worried about was something like this happening."

"I had everything under control."

"Yeah. Right. Well, bust my buns for worrying that someone, other than me, would get hurt."

"Bust your...*what?*" Without meaning to, her gaze slipped down to the tight curve of his jeans. The backside of his jeans. She laughed self-consciously and looked away.

Gabe snorted; Chase gave in to one small smile.

Yet, the implication was clear. He was worried about her, worried she'd get hurt. Though he'd said it before, this time the knowledge warmed Mallory and made her fondness for him grow, even without her wanting it to. "You have to trust me," she chided. "Trust me to know that I am doing the right thing with that animal where she is concerned."

He gazed down at her and the light in his silver gaze softened.

The momentary look they shared must have startled Gabe, and embarrassed him, because he harrumphed to remind them of his presence. "Well, I'll saddle up," he offered. "See if I can round her up or drive her back to the barns. She's gonna be a piece of work now. Now that she's got a little fresh air in her lungs."

"I'll open the gate to the corral," Chase said, dragging his gaze away from Mallory. "See if we can get her in there. It'll have to do. She'll never let us within fifteen feet of her."

"Neither of you have to do anything," Mallory protested. "I let her get away from me, I'll take care of it."

"Mallory..."

"Ma'am, roundin' that horse up could take half the day," Gabe warned. "Me and Tony'll—'

"You could at least let me try," she interrupted.

The men exchanged looks. Indulgent looks.

"Sure. Go ahead if you want," Chase finally said, his arms relaxing at his sides.

Summoning her courage, Mallory pivoted and walked

away from the men, following the direction Peggy Sue had taken. When she was twenty feet ahead of the men, and with her eye fixed on the animal that still ran free two hundred yards ahead of her, she put two fingers between her teeth and let out a shrill whistle.

Peggy Sue slowed to a trot.

Mallory whistled again.

Peggy Sue's determination obviously lagged, and she hesitated, then circled back to face Mallory. With the lush valley at her backside, and myriad confining barns and small circle of the corral facing her, the horse's indecision was tangible.

Mallory whistled a third time.

Peggy Sue slowly retraced her steps, picking up speed, and finally come back to the yard at a trot. She ran right up to Mallory and stilled, her sides quivering, her nostrils wide and distended.

Mallory reclaimed the lead. "Peggy Sue," she whispered, running her hand down the horse's sweaty neck, "you can't do that, baby. Not ever again. I was afraid I'd lose you. I was afraid you'd never come back to me. And we'd both lose so much then. You wouldn't ever be able to go home…and as for me…well…I told you, I have my reasons, too."

Peggy Sue, weary from the run and unused to such physical exercise, heaved.

Behind her, Mallory recognized the excited disbelief in Gabe's young voice.

"Didja see that? How'd she do that?"

She turned back to see Chase shaking his head, a bemused expression haunting his chiseled features.

It struck her then how much she was keeping from him.

It was disturbing, almost painful, because she felt compelled to share everything with him. But she couldn't tell him *everything*...certainly not about this animal, and certainly not what she carried in her heart.

Chapter Eight

Chase eyed the recliner regretfully, then lowered his aching body onto the straight-backed kitchen chair. It was better for his ribs. Heck of a way for a man to have to sit and think, not being able to lean back and ponder like he wanted.

Of course, he'd never figured he was much of a pondering man, anyway. But Mallory sure had changed things—suddenly all he was doing was thinking about the past, and the future, and the mess he'd made out of the present.

Until she'd come along, he'd been perfectly content to glide along, work like a slave from sunrise to sundown, then fall into bed at midnight and welcome an exhausted sleep. His house had been quiet, and he'd embraced that solitude. He'd quit listening long ago for the rush of tiny footsteps running down the hall. He'd quit listening for the tinkle of a music box that played "It's a Small World." He'd quit hoping to once again hear the petulant refrain of a three-year-old's "Daddy!" He'd closed the door to the nursery and turned it into some kind of slipshod storeroom.

On an adult level, he hadn't found comfort in his bed for years. What possessed him to think he could find it there now?

Mallory. The name rolled through his head like a craving. Or a taunt.

He snorted. Get real, Wells. Mallory Chevalle was out of his league. If he had a hankering for a woman, he'd be far better off to pay for a bed by the hour. No commitments, no ties, just pure physical relief.

Of course, that had never been his style—never had been, never would be—but there was a certain appeal...to just letting his mind wander, and savor, all the intimacies life offered.

When he was twenty he'd loved lying next to a woman. They smelled sweet, seductive...

And, in his recollection, no one had ever smelled sweeter than Mallory. Now, most days, when she sat on the bed with him, she smelled like this intoxicating combination of sweet clover and honey—with a crazy dash of kitchen vanilla thrown in.

He'd once thought nothing could be so warm as a woman, especially in those early morning hours—after a man had discovered just how soft she could be the night before.

And Mallory touched him with a penetrating heat. As she checked his gauze bandages or smoothed ointment onto his sores, her heat seemed to coil through and into him, putting a smoldering fire into his loins.

But even from his youth, he'd always recognized that it was a woman's voice that could fire his senses. One intoxicating laugh. The softest of sighs. The quivery little sound they made when they knew they were vulnerable.

And right now, Mallory was the most vulnerable woman he knew. He looked at her so often and wondered what it

would be like to be the first man to introduce her to intimacy. The only man, a man strong enough, yet tender
enough, to win her. To stroke her warm, moist curves, to
draw kittenish sounds from the back of her throat, to hear
her laugh with pleasure, to writhe with the first thrust of
pain. To teach her about a wonderful new world that existed
between man and woman.

God, what was he thinking? He was going crazy. He was
nuttier than that dang horse she was trying to tame.

Chase raked his fingers through his hair and tried to beat
back the memories.

He should take a good hard lesson from his life, that's
what. Sharon had made one thing perfectly clear: his bed
was nothing more than a place to hang his hat and sleep.

He'd done the commitment thing once and it had been
a fiasco. From beginning to end. But, he reminded himself,
how was Mallory to know that?

Every time she was solicitous, how could she know
Sharon turned her back? Every time she laughed, how
could she know that Sharon had only smiled grimly, as if
she was indulging him, nothing more. How could she know
that the wealth she discounted was something Sharon had
yearned for, coveted?

At the end, Sharon had been tight-lipped and wearisome.
Maybe they both had been, he conceded. They'd had good-
enough reason.

So many differences—and all of them smashing head-
long into one another.

Yet…Mallory didn't just talk, she had this animated little
chirp in her voice. She didn't treat the hired hands like
servants, she regarded them as friends. She was vibrant and
full of life.

Sometimes he'd look at her and think she had these little
stars in her eyes—stars that just seemed to glow from

within her own little backdrop of baby blue heaven. Of course, he could read what those stars spelled out: innocence, sincerity, hope. All lined up, like some spectacular planetary formation, all committed to the belief that the man-woman bond would cure all evil and right all wrong.

Sure, she was different than Sharon. But a woman's internal drive never changed.

He had to get his head on straight and get over it. Now, before his heart kept prodding him in the wrong direction.

Lewt poked his head in the kitchen. "You looked out the back door lately?"

"No."

"Might want to come take a look at this."

Chase stared down in annoyance at his boots. He was having a devil of a time pulling them on, and he had the distinct impression Mallory had intentionally left him in the lurch this morning and hurried out to the barns. He hated himself for being increasingly dependant on all the thoughtful things she did for him.

"Be there in a minute," he growled, wedging his elbow against his ribs and sinking two incisors into his bottom lip. He'd pull the blasted things on no matter what, even if he cracked another rib doing it.

Tony swaggered into the room. "Hey, boss, that little *señorita*'s a handful, eh?"

Chase lifted his eyes and poked his toe into the shaft of his boot. The boot twisted out from under him. Frustration and pain made Chase groan.

"Need a little help, boss?" Tony offered, striding over.

Lewt snickered; Chase glared up at him.

After several clumsy attempts they managed to get his boots on, and Chase levered himself out of the chair.

"Thanks," he grumbled. "I don't know what's the matter with me, must've slept wrong or something."

"No wonder. I don't know how you stand it, havin' a woman like that sleepin' under the same roof with you. If it was me," Tony confided, his dark eyes teasing, "and I had one cracked rib? Hell, I'd risk another just to get at her."

The statement, a man's joke Tony might have uttered six months ago without eliciting much attention, now rankled. Chase concentrated on stuffing the hem of his shirt into his jeans. "That's the difference between you and me," Chase muttered, "I'm not a man that puts out to stud."

"Nope. The difference—" Tony winked "—is that drop of Spanish blood. We're lovers, not fighters."

Chase ignored him and grabbed his hat off the table before he caught Lewt's speculative look. He paused. "So," he asked. "What's up?"

"Take a look-see," Lewt said, inclining his head.

Chase walked past him and to the back door, where the corral was in full view. Mallory was putting Peggy Sue through her paces, and Gabe was hanging on the corral fence, transfixed.

The pit of Chase's stomach roiled. "That horse isn't ready yet, not to be—"

"Let's go outside," Lewt said.

"Boss, that woman is really somethin'," Tony remarked. "She knows more'n just handlin' horseflesh. She knows how to *talk* to 'em."

The reverence with which Tony framed the last sentence made Chase stop and look at him. He wasn't serious? Was he?

"Damnedest thing," Lewt agreed. "Talks to Peggy Sue just like she understands. Heard of them horse whisperers before. Never rightly saw one, though."

"She's not a horse whisperer!" Chase retorted. "She's just—" he shrugged "—she's just got her own style, that's all."

Tony and Lewt exchanged looks.

"What! What is that supposed to mean?"

"The gal's got an instinct," Lewt allowed. "Like she knows somethin', somethin' more'n the rest of us."

"Sometimes—if I didn't know better, boss—I'd think that horse was talkin' back to her. You can just see it. Like they're carryin' a conversation."

Chase momentarily regarded Tony. "The only thing that ever seems to be working around here is your Spanish imagination," he grumbled. But he couldn't help it...his eyes were drawn to the corral, where Mallory led Peggy Sue in a wide circle. Their progress was slow, sometimes stop-start, but she *did* have her on a lead, and Peggy Sue offered little resistance.

As if he were drawn to the scene, Chase moved out of the house and down the back porch stairs. Lewt and Tony followed.

"Peggy Sue's probably just taken with her," Chase said to no one in particular. "Horses are like that sometimes. We all have our favorites."

"Yup," Lewt agreed. "Most likely. Gabe, now? He swears she's got the gift."

"Gabe's still a kid," Chase replied. "He's impressionable, he's—"

They were fifty feet away when a flash of orange suddenly whirled atop one of the corral fenceposts. Peggy Sue saw it and jumped. The lead rope went taut, and Mallory automatically braced, refusing to let the horse pull away.

Pumpkin, the cat, settled in on top of the post, feigning disinterest in the fracas she'd caused. She nonchalantly curled her fat orange tail around her legs, then assumed a three-legged stance and licked one front paw.

The breath seemed to leave Chase, and he stalled. They all did. They were all afraid to move.

Every one of those men knew what that horse was capable of. She'd use any excuse to rampage. Even a barn cat.

Yet it was Mallory who was alone with her in the corral. Mallory who sidled close to her and put a hand on her neck. Mallory who coaxed her forward.

Chase's heart thrummed wildly. He could feel the blood rushing through his veins, he could hear it pounding in his ears. This crazy mixture of fear and anticipation, of hope and dread. He desperately wanted Mallory to succeed, and yet he was half afraid she would.

Then what? What would he do then?

There was no logical explanation for any of this. None at all. Mallory handled Peggy Sue easily, as if she were little more than a skittish colt. Every one of them knew that wasn't the case. That horse was hell on wheels.

Chase watched in fascination as Peggy Sue reluctantly inched closer. Her piercing gaze never drifted from Pumpkin.

Mallory said something to her, but he couldn't hear what.

Peggy Sue shook her head but took another step closer. Then another. And another…until she stood a mere yard from Pumpkin.

The taming of the shrew, Chase thought absurdly.

His limbs tensed and his mind raced. He half expected Peggy Sue to bolt or—worse—charge. Mallory would be tossed up against the fence like a rag doll and knocked senseless.

He didn't dare intervene, but the strained silence and forced inactivity pressed down on him like a weight. The

GET FREE BOOKS and a FREE GIFT WHEN YOU PLAY THE...

Just scratch off the silver box with a coin. Then check below to see the gifts you get!

SLOT MACHINE GAME!

YES! I have scratched off the silver box. Please send me the 2 free Silhouette Romance® books and gift for which I qualify. I understand I am under no obligation to purchase any books, as explained on the back of this card.

315 SDL DQLM

215 SDL DRNJ
(S-R-11/02)

FIRST NAME	LAST NAME

ADDRESS

APT.#	CITY

STATE/PROV.	ZIP/POSTAL CODE

7	7	7	**Worth TWO FREE BOOKS plus a BONUS Mystery Gift!**
🍒	🍒	🍒	**Worth TWO FREE BOOKS!**
♣	♣	♣	**Worth ONE FREE BOOK!**
🔔	🔔	🍒	**TRY AGAIN!**

Visit us online at www.eHarlequin.com

DETACH AND MAIL CARD TODAY!

The Silhouette Reader Service™ — Here's how it works:

Accepting your 2 free books and gift places you under no obligation to buy anything. You may keep the books and gift and return the shipping statement marked "cancel." If you do not cancel, about a month later we'll send you 6 additional novels and bill you just $3.34 each in the U.S., or $3.80 each in Canada, plus 25¢ shipping & handling per book and applicable taxes if any.* That's the complete price and — compared to cover prices of $3.99 each in the U.S. and $4.50 each in Canada — it's quite a bargain! You may cancel at any time, but if you choose to continue, every month we'll send you 6 more books, which you may either purchase at the discount price or return to us and cancel your subscription.

*Terms and prices subject to change without notice. Sales tax applicable in N.Y. Canadian residents will be charged applicable provincial taxes and GST.

men around him were equally grim, equally apprehensive. Gabe slowly, imperceptibly, peeled himself off the fence. Lewt's leathery wrinkles deepened as his eyes narrowed, and his mouth went grim. Tony's fingers flexed, as if he was preparing to spring into action.

It struck him then. How they were all preparing to save this woman, this fair foreign damsel, from destruction. But it didn't happen.

Pumpkin stood, arching her back, her tail high in the air. Then she leapt down to the fence rail and padded away. Peggy Sue curiously watched her departure.

A collective sigh of relief emanated from the men.

Mallory offered Peggy Sue a blinding smile and encouraging words. Together, they turned back into the center of the corral, and when the men had reassembled to watch, they faced them.

Mallory's animated face glowed, with what Chase likened to a heavenly light. He thought of her floating out of her convertible that first day; he thought of her bending over him when he was flat on his back in the alley next to Peggy Sue's stall; he thought of her ministrations with his bandages, with his medicine—and with his boots.

He'd once dubbed her an angel. Lewt suggested she was a horse whisperer. Tony carried on about her talking to the animals as if she were Dr. Dolittle's daughter. Gabe figured she had a gift.

Mallory Chevalle…so many things to so many people.

A drive to possess this multifaceted woman burned deep inside Chase. Her innocent beauty filled him with a heady desire he was grappling to control. Reminders of her kisses made him go tight with want, with need.

Yet his rational mind was brutal, abrupt and unforgiving.

Logic reminded him too many things were keeping them apart. One ugly divorce. One lost child. And a horse named Peggy Sue.

It was eleven o'clock at night, and Chase was dawdling. He'd put off going to bed, mostly because he knew Mallory would be behind a closed door, across the hall from him. An hour ago, he'd heard the shower running and he'd thought of her in it. He'd thought of her using his towels...and his soap. He thought of that one lucky, slippery bar of soap touching all the places he wanted to touch.

He was going half goofy with all these disturbing thoughts. It wasn't enough the woman had invaded his home, now she'd invaded his mind.

He paired his boots by his favorite kitchen chair, turned off the overhead light, then reluctantly padded upstairs in his stocking feet. Behind her closed door, he could hear the faint strains of a country-western radio station. They were playing a provocatively sensual song, and the lyrics seemed to curl from beneath the door and draw him into their magical hold. A song about lovers, and being held in the cold, lonely night. A song of seduction.

Chase paused. He reckoned it would have taken a team of horses to prevent his arm from rising, his knuckles from rapping on the oak door frame.

"Just a minute." Mallory's voice did a crazy duet with the mesmerizing music. In seconds, she opened the door and peered around it. "Is everything okay?" she asked, her brow slightly furrowed as she slid a cursory gaze down his length.

"Fine. I wanted to thank you for today."

She looked momentarily confused.

"For what you did with Peggy Sue. For the progress you've made." The spaghetti straps of her gown were loose over her shoulder.

The unexpected praise seemed to relax her and the door

swung open farther, revealing the curvy side of her breast, the sweetheart neckline of her gown.

"Oh. That." She smiled. "You told me that already."

"I know…but…I was thinking about it, and…." He trailed off.

Her toes curled into the nappy rug, then flicked against the bottom of the door. She had cherry-red polish on her toenails.

Huh. That ought to tell him something.

"Me, too, Chase," she said softly. "I was thinking about this afternoon, too. The way you looked at me. I saw this…this funny look in your eyes…like you didn't believe it. Or maybe you didn't want to believe it."

He lifted a shoulder.

"She's getting better, Chase. Every day she's getting better."

"I know. I can see it." He leaned against the door frame, the first time he'd been able to do that in days without his sides killing him. "How'd you manage that, Mallory? What are your special powers? What allows you to do what every cowboy on this ranch has failed at?"

Her smile was Mona Lisa magic, and it hovered on her lips, mysteriously inviting, tempting him with his own human frailties. He wanted her so much, he could almost feel his body reaching for her. Every cell went to pitch-point alert, even as his head and all his rational thoughts went dizzily out of control.

"I believe," she said softly, her words a haunting reminder. "I believe that Peggy Sue has been waiting for someone like me and that I can help her. That's all. I believe."

He stared at her as an idea sprung into his head. "I believe in certain things, too," he said. "Like recognizing people when they deserve it. Like celebrating when it's called for.'' She inclined her head. ''We've got a reason to celebrate, Mallory. You've taken that horse further than anyone could imagine. The Horseshoe Falls Haydays starts tomorrow. How about if we both take the day off? I think we deserve it.''

Mallory debated. ''I don't know. I really should spend every second with Peggy Sue, especially now.''

''You can't rush her,'' Chase pointed out.

''But it might be too much for you.''

''I'm the one extending the invitation, Mallory. I'd be pleased if you'd accept. It's Wyoming hospitality, and it's something you ought to be introduced to.''

''Before I leave?'' she asked softly.

The thought of her leaving torpedoed through his mind, leaving a big, black, empty hole. ''Yeah. I guess. Can't quite imagine you leaving, though. Things'll be kind of quiet around here without you stirring them up.''

''I'll just have to go back to Narwhal and stir them up.'' She smiled. ''Have you ever been to Europe, Chase? Or Narwhal?''

''Years ago, I spent a week in Germany, with my mom.''

''Narwhal's a little more...exotic. But you'd like it. The invitation's always open, Chase. For you to be my guest.''

They both stood there, silently, letting time hang unrecognized between them. Both thinking private thoughts. Both yearning.

She was lithe and lovely.

He was strong and straightforward.

''So...about tomorrow...?''

''I'd love to. Really.''

He felt himself break into a giant, relieved smile. Just like a teenager. ''Great.''

Their eyes caught and held. Neither one wanted to let go. Oh, if they could be frozen this way for an eternity, it would be the closest to paradise as they could ever allow themselves to get.

It was Chase, and his human, male need that broke away first. "I know you kiss boo-boos," he said, "but do you give out good-night kisses, too? You know, something to sleep on?"

The question obviously surprised her. "I..."

"It's not such a big thing, Mallory," he said huskily.

She looked up at him, with the biggest, bluest eyes he'd ever seen in his whole life. Eyes that were full of trust yet simmering with need. She silently nudged the door aside and reached up to hook an arm around the back of his neck and draw him nearer to her. He was so much taller than she that she had to stand on her tiptoes. "I don't want to hurt you," she breathed.

"You aren't, the only hurt is—" he broke off, his mouth claiming hers, the taste of her lips reminiscent of honey, the touch of her tongue as seductive as velvet "—wanting you...." He whispered the words against her mouth, before deepening the kiss.

Mallory sighed and pressed against him, the satin gown twisting over her breasts and stretching taut over the curve of her hip. The softness of her belly molded to his middle, her abdomen cradling the heat of his passion.

She moaned, the kittenish sounds translating to pure pleasure.

Instinct kicked in. He sought her breast, raking his palm over the side of her ribs, before he held its heavy weight and stroked it, his thumb venturing nearer the peak. He barely grazed the nubile point when she gasped, her head arching back. He followed, planting kisses on the warm pulse points along her neck, and lower, to the hollow of her throat.

Rasping need shuddered through her, and he pulled her

closer. Tactilely, he discovered her softness, with deft strokes and intimate caresses. He wanted to kiss her there so much it became almost a litany in his head, to push himself closer, to take a greater chance.

"Chase…?"

In the recesses of his mind, his name was distorted, and agony mingled with pleasure. She writhed against him, and suddenly his hands were full of her. One arm looped the small of her back, one hand captured and settled on the whole of her breast, knowing its firmness, its full, questing peak. He was brimming over with desire.

Then the realization hit him like a ton of bricks.

He was touching someone who had never been touched. He was leading someone where she shouldn't go. Not with him. Not with someone who couldn't cherish this gift for an eternity.

He broke away, his hands sliding uselessly away from her comforting body. "Mallory, I—I let things get out of control. I—"

She looked at him, dazed, incomprehension making her features go slack. "Don't," she said. "Don't apologize."

He looked at her sharply.

"Perhaps you've educated my little virgin soul." She tried to laugh, but her attempt at humor was pitiful. "About all the things that I want to happen…and all the things that can't." She put a respectable distance between them. "It's okay, Chase. It's just something we won't ever let happen again."

Chapter Nine

Horseshoe Falls was the place to be. The town was full of dusty pickups, big-haired cowgirls and tobacco-chewing cowboys. Horses—an acceptable mode of transportation for the weekend celebration—nimbly negotiated the hubbub of activity, and no one looked twice. The heavy, sweet smell of cooking wafted through the streets.

Chase paused before a food trailer. "How about an elephant ear?" he asked Mallory.

She blinked in surprise.

He couldn't help it. He laughed, right out loud...and doing so felt so good he barely noticed the ache in his ribs. "It's a pastry," he explained, "with powdered sugar and cinnamon. Or strawberries, if you want."

She mimicked the stance of other cowgirls on the street and stood with her new, flamingo-pink boots planted in the sawdust as she rocked back on her heels. "Powdered sugar," she decreed.

Chase ordered, paid for it, then extended the paper plate to Mallory. She broke off a piece of the elephant ear, tentatively bit into the warm, crisp crust and immediately broke into a smile. "Wonderful," she breathed. "It is like *bourlainne,* my father's favorite pastry."

He smiled and broke off a piece for himself. "I imagine we have a lot of things that aren't so different."

"My, I wish there was time," she said, "for you to introduce me to them all."

Chase didn't hear the first part, only the second. He had this hankering to introduce her to so much, to introduce her to a whole new world of pleasure and experience. Trying not to think of it, he gestured to the carnival rides at the end of the block and ushered her toward them. "Do you have things like this in Narwhal?"

They strolled together in the middle of the street, contentedly brushing shoulders as they shared the pastry. "We have Celebration of Days. There are soccer games instead of rodeos, and parades with Narwhal's officials in traditional dress. There are horses and carriages. We have wine instead of beer. And people come from all over the world to see the pageant."

"The pageant?"

"We have a pageant honoring the legend of the unicorn. Narwhal, if you remember, means unicorn of the sea."

The last thing Chase wanted to talk about were unicorns and legends. Not today. He made a point of looking at the Tilt-A-Whirl. A couple laughed giddily as they were thrown against each other. He wondered how it would be, to be pressed against Mallory, to feel her body bumping his, her flesh softening against his side.

His ribs couldn't take that kind of impact—but his heart could.

Mallory watched intently, too, and he wondered vaguely if she wanted to ride with him on something that was spinning merrily out of control. Not like they weren't, he thought wryly as he thought of the kiss and the touches they had shared the previous evening.

They moved on, past the fun house, where a towheaded kid bumped into a jumble of mirrors, and a little girl in pigtails skipped over a swinging bridge.

They finished the pastry and Chase made a detour to get them a fresh-squeezed lemonade. He'd started to order them each one, but Mallory stopped him, her hand on his arm. "Let's share," she said softly. "Or…you can just give me a taste."

His gaze drifted lazily to her mouth, and he considered the implications. The intimacy of it, the thought of her shell-pink lipstick on the rim, the crushed ice brushing her mouth…and then brushing his. He'd ordered a large to make the experience last as long as humanly possible.

He'd offered it to her first.

"Ah, so many good things," she said, the tip of her tongue swiping her mouth before offering it back.

He lifted a shoulder and took a drink. "I guess. I'd forgotten. It's been so long since I've been here."

"Really?"

"Mmm." He steered her forward, to the Himalaya, consciously aware that he didn't want to explain the reasons for his absence from the Horseshoe Falls Haydays. "That was my favorite ride when I was a teenager," he said, pointing with the lemonade cup. The music blared and cars of riders picked up speed, disappearing behind garishly painted scenes of snow-covered mountains, then momentarily reappeared, clutching the safety bars, their hair flying. "Once," he qualified. "When I was a kid, and my ribs didn't hurt."

"It won't hurt forever, Chase."

He stared at her, wondering if she knew how prophetic her words were…for he'd heard a different meaning and he was beginning to believe in the possibility of it. They moved on and, without intending to, paused at the kiddie rides.

Frazzled parents were laughing, even as they ushered their toddlers onto tiny trains and whirling airplanes. One exuberant little girl waved at them, and Chase felt his heart wrench. Without thinking, he put his arm around Mallory, possessively snagging the belt loop on her jeans with his thumb. She looked up at him and tucked herself under his arm and against his shoulder.

God, it was a good feeling. So very, very good. He missed it, and he wanted it back.

Together they turned and walked away, before the emotions of want crowded into his mind, making him question what they were doing and why they were doing it.

They paused at the end of the midway, at the foot of the huge Ferris wheel. Dusk was settling, and the yellow-and-white tube lights were just beginning to glow. "Now, that's a ride that wouldn't hurt my ribs."

Mallory lifted her head, taking in the swinging seat at the very top. "If we were up there, I could see forever."

Without asking, Chase promptly bought two tickets. "Maybe not forever," he said, offering them to her, "but at least a little piece of Wyoming."

They tossed the empty lemonade cup in the trash and boarded the Ferris wheel, settling onto the red vinyl-covered seat. The attendant lowered the bar, latching it, and the strangest sense of intimacy encapsulated Chase. As if they were shutting the world out…as if this was just their experience, for the two of them, to be shared and savored.

The attendant stepped back and hit the button. The great wheel moved, and the seat swung back from the momentum. Mallory caught her breath and flattened her shoulder blades against the back of the seat.

"I don't know why I did this. These things scare me," she said.

"Scare you?" Chase repeated, his eyes fastened only on Mallory as he ignored the hurried scene below. The cacophony of sounds faded to a soothing rush of air. "I didn't think anything scared you."

She chuckled. "You give me too much credit."

"Hey. I've seen you look that crazy Peggy Sue in the eye and not back down one inch." They were halfway to the top, and the wind riffled through her hair, tossing an errant strand across her cheek.

Mallory clutched the bar and ventured a cautious look out across the grounds.

Chase did the most natural thing in the world: he picked the spun-gold strand of hair from her cheek and carefully hooked it behind her ear. Mallory gave him a sideways look and smiled her thanks.

The moment pulled at his heartstrings.

"I'm scared of a lot of things, Chase," she said softly as the ride stopped just before the top. The gondola swung in its hinges, and Chase automatically moved close and slipped his arm around her shoulders. "I'm scared I won't be able to take Peggy Sue as far as I want. To teach her as much as I want."

"C'mon."

"No. It's true." She tilted her head, moving closer within his embrace. "And I worry about my father. His health is failing," she confided. "And I worry what I will do if something happens to him. It scares me, more than I've ever admitted. Not to anyone," she said. "Even with all his advisers, I'll be alone. The decisions for the shipping company would rest solely on my shoulders. And there is so much to be responsible for." She sighed, pausing thoughtfully. "And," she said softly, "I love him. If you think I am brave, it is because of him. He has taught me so much. He wants me to pursue my own life, yet I regret every day we are apart.''

"Is he why you talked about going home last night?''

"Mostly. I always feel—'' she hesitated, then the Ferris wheel started up again, moving slowly, putting them closer to the top "—as if I should find the one thing that can give him comfort.''

"That's why you wanted the horse,'' Chase observed. "To amuse him.''

"No. No, it is more than that,'' she protested as the wheel sailed up to the top. "I'm looking for that thing that will bring him peace. Especially in his final days.''

Final days. The memories assaulted Chase and he tried to repulse them—but it was too late and he couldn't beat them back. A nappy stuffed horse, with a mane and tail of blunt-cut white yarn. A tattered yellow blanket. A red velveteen dress. For a cowboy's hardened heart, it seemed strange it was only the soft things he remembered.

"As a father—'' He cleared his throat, willing the lump away, and started again. "I imagine he'll know the greatest contentment if you are well and happy.''

"Of course that is what he says, but...'' Mallory shrugged, and seemed to relax in the circle of his arm. She dragged her gaze away to survey the glittering lights of the midway and the town of Horseshoe Falls. "I feel driven to give him something more.''

"I understand.''

She turned to him, and her hand briefly moved to his chest, to flutter lightly across the region of his heart. "I hope so. I truly hope that some day you understand.''

The moment of intimate thoughts and gestures passed. The wheel moved and brought them down in the vortex of people who milled on the ground; it revolved and they made a swirling dash in and out of reality.

Heaven and hell, Chase thought wryly. Over the top, and into the briefest glimpse of heaven, and then down, into the everyday humdrum of hell.

After several minutes, they floated down, and Chase intuitively knew the ride was over. Given the regretful expression on her face, apparently Mallory knew it, too.

"Thank you, Chase," she whispered. "For everything. For tonight, and for letting me tell you about my father and all. I trust you, Chase Wells. With everything that's nearest and dearest to my heart."

They were within ten feet of the ground, and Chase knew he had to put a tight rein on his feelings. There was no alternative. Not with his past and her uncertain future. He chuckled, and it sounded a little too loud to his own ears. "You've been watching too much American TV," he chided, "saying things like that."

A flicker of surprise, maybe even hurt, rolled through Mallory's eyes, but she said nothing and simply put her hand in his when they exited the gondola.

They walked like that, in silence, to the end of the midway. Hand in hand, their hearts speaking volumes, their heads filled with private thoughts. Maybe they each knew time was running out, Chase thought bitterly, maybe they each were trying to make it last as long as they possibly could.

"Let's go over to Main Street," he said gruffly. "They always have stuff going on over there."

They did—and it was a street dance.

The street was barricaded off, and all the storefronts, except for Dilly's Tavern and The Leather Chaps Café, were dark. Colored lights were strung over the street, puncturing the blue velvet backdrop. Couples were rocking to the "Boot Scootin' Boogie," while a long-neck bottle of beer rested against many hips.

They stood on the sidelines, and Mallory watched in fascination. Her hand was still safely clasped in his, and he leaned closer, bending her arm across the small of her back, to tuck her possessively against his side.

"You dance?" he asked.

"Not like this."

He grinned down at her.

"My father saw that I was well schooled in dance. I have been known to waltz the night away," she said proudly.

"Ah...the *slow* dance," he emphasized. "Of course, out here, we put our own spin on it." As if preordained, the band broke into a crooning, country-western piece. "My kind of music," he approved. "Shall we?"

Mallory glanced skeptically at the crowd, then pushed aside her indecision and stepped down from the curb and onto the street. Who knew? This could be her only chance to be with a man she admired as much as Chase. She had certainly danced with her share of dumpy old men, or flamboyant full-of-themselves young ones. Tonight was her chance to experience Chase Wells and his life. She'd be a fool to turn her back on it. For a memory lasted forever.

She turned and demurely put one hand just above his waist, at his back, and extended the other, gracefully, as she had been taught.

Chase looked at her, as if she were posing, a hint of amusement on his features. "Uh-uh. Not here, honey." He gently snagged her wrist from his back and removed it, then captured her other free-floating one. Wincing slightly from the effort, he looped her arms around his neck.

A ripple of shock went through her when his arms wound around her, settling on the curve of her back, to drag her up against his chest.

"But so close," she exclaimed, whispering, and slightly pulling back.

"So?"

"Everyone is looking."

He chuckled. "Not here, honey. They're all too busy doing the same thing."

Mallory covertly glanced around her, then over Chase's shoulder. Yes. This was the way of the slow dance in Horseshoe Falls. Cowboy hats bobbed and tipped, shielding couples from prying eyes. Bodies swayed as one, moving in sync with the haunting melody.

Knowing the dance was accepted, and nothing extraordinary, Mallory felt herself relax and warm inside Chase's arms. Rational thought grew fuzzy as her forefinger absently traced the back yoke of his shirt...the shirt she had laundered only a few days ago. It was a disturbing pull, deep on the inside, to possess such intimate knowledge about Chase—the last snap on the shirtfront was broken, the tag had been cut from inside the collar, and the hem was frayed.

The music lulled her, and she felt him move closer as his head tipped down and the brim of his hat blocked the romantic, twinkling lights from view. Without realizing it, she closed her eyes and let every sensation rule. Her determination to resist emotion crumbled.

He smelled so good. He made her feel so good. Everything was so right.

Her heart pitched with a force she had never before experienced.

Her father claimed sharing the parameters of marriage with another offered incomparable joy. She wondered.

Her father had never understood her determination to keep suitors at arm's length. Of course, her father was unaware of her need to remain chaste to fulfill the legend. It was something she had dreamed of since she was a small child.

And now there was Chase Wells…who loved his horses and his wild life of freedom on the rugged Wyoming ranchland. A man's man, one who stood independent and tall, one who was firm in conviction and had the soul to choose what was right.

She wondered what her father would think of him. Intuitively, she knew he would approve. Knowing that made her heart melt a little bit more.

The music ended, but Mallory was lost to a whirlwind of sensation that swept the remnants of her resistance away and filled her with a lethargy. Inside, she felt heavy and pliable. Her mind was numb to anything but Chase.

"You're pretty light on your feet there," Chase remarked.

Mallory chuckled and leaned back to look up at him. Doing so made her legs sluice between his, fusing their middles. She became acutely aware they were conjoined with need. "It doesn't feel that way," she confided.

He snorted and practically gathered her up in his arms. She had the distinct impression he'd lift her and swing her off her feet, if his ribs would allow it.

The next piece, another slow song, started playing. Both Mallory and Chase automatically moved to the music.

Suddenly, without warning, a hand clapped Chase on the back. Just enough to make him wince. "Good to see you, Chase," a deep voice boomed. "Even better to see you dancing again."

Chase pivoted and smiled. "Grant."

"Yessir. The last time I saw you out here dancing it was with Skylar."

Mallory felt Chase stiffen. From the corner of her eye,

she saw him clench his jaw, and the smile drop from his face.

The broad-shouldered cowboy didn't seem to notice. "And this would be?" he said easily.

"Mallory Chevalle. She's my guest for a few days while she's looking at stock," Chase explained. "Mallory, meet Grant Maxwell. He runs the livestock auction outside of town. Who knows? Maybe *he's* got a horse to sell you."

Mallory laughed.

"Prob'ly not," Grant admitted. "We pretty much have the swayback, put-it-out-to-pasture variety. Got an auction comin' up in a coupla weeks, though, Chase. You ought to come by."

"Maybe."

Grant's eyes narrowed perceptively, and he nodded. "Been a long time, big guy. Of course, I'm just glad to see you out and about." He offered Chase a firm handshake, then winked at Mallory. "You take care of him, now, you hear?"

Chapter Ten

Chase's demeanor changed drastically after the meeting with Grant Maxwell. They danced a couple of more dances, then he suggested they head back, saying his side was bothering him. Given that he rarely complained about the pain, Mallory suspected it was more than that.

She glanced back over her shoulder to the street dance, to the simple little place where she had left a piece of her heart behind and regretted that the night was over too soon. She had never danced on asphalt before, only inlaid floors. She had never danced beneath strings of colored lights, only chandeliers.

They walked slowly to the truck, saying nothing.

The cool night air made Mallory more conscious of her heated, damp skin. "I should have brought a jacket," she commented idly.

Chase didn't reply, then he jerked open the truck door and yanked out a torn flannel shirt. He shoved it in her direction. "Best I can do."

Mallory momentarily stared at it, imagining Chase's

arms around her instead. Wondering what had happened that changed things so. She took the shirt and pulled it over her arms, shouldering it up. "Thank you."

The oddest expression lurked behind Chase's gray eyes. Finally, he reached over and straightened the collar, pulling it free as his fingers skimmed the pulse point of her neck. Her blood quickened. "My poor little rich girl," he mused, "I'm dressing you up in rags."

In spite of her discomfort with his mood, Mallory laughed. "I don't care. It's been wonderful just to be with you. To see this side of you."

Chase looked away and quickly fumbled with the truck keys in his hand.

"Chase? What's the matter?" Her hand caught his wrist, drawing his attention back where it needed to be—on them, on this moment. "Is it something I did? Or said?"

A flicker of surprise made his jaw slide off center. "No. No, I didn't mean for you to think that...." He looked away in the direction of the bright lights and the faint sounds of music and wild laughter they'd left behind.

"Chase, I...get the impression you're mad. At me."

"At you?" His words were tinged with disbelief. "No. No, not you. I'm mad at myself, maybe. For remembering. Seems like there's times I can't help it. Or people remind me."

"Remind you of someone else?" she asked quietly, carefully. "Of...Skylar?"

The vestiges of a smile turned his mouth. "Yeah," he finally admitted, "Skylar."

A flash of jealousy punctured Mallory's heart. She didn't mean for it to happen, it just did. She wished she could beat it back. Hadn't there been others in his life? Hadn't he told her he was experienced?

"But it isn't what you think," he said softly. He let the

truck door fall shut, but not quite closed. Then he hunched forward, wedging both elbows on the sides of the truck, as his hands dangled inside over the truck bed.

"How could you possibly know what I think?" Though she hated it, she heard the hysterical, possessive rise of her voice.

He looked over his shoulder at her, and in the light of a full moon, she could see him grin.

"I'm sorry," she said quickly. "I'm sounding…petulant. Daddy hates it when I sound like that. It makes me sound spoiled and mean and—"

"Shh." He silenced her by swiveling his three middle fingers. "No, don't say that. You're anything but. Maybe I needed to hear it. To remind myself there's a past and a present." His fingers drifted lazily from her mouth. "I haven't told you about my past, Mallory, because I didn't think there was a need."

Mallory's heart raced. Chase was a man who didn't share a confidence—not unless he trusted you. She waited, breathlessly.

"Skylar was my little girl," he said softly. "My only child. My daughter." He straightened, pushing off the truck. "She was born with a congenital heart defect and she died two years ago, when she was three."

Mallory went weak, and a chill rushed over her arms. There had been no indication a child had ever been in that house. Not one. "You had a child," she said, numbly realizing that if there had been a child, there would have had to be a wife. Maybe there still was one.

"You never guessed."

She shook her head.

"I married Sharon seven years ago, and if I do to say so myself, it was a pretty amicable event. But I'll be the first to admit that immediately after we said 'I do' things went downhill. Sharon was the classic version of the 'back east' girl marrying the 'out West' cowboy. She wanted the cowboy, all right. She just didn't know what to do with him after she got him.''

When Mallory offered him a sympathetic smile; he looked away.

"I thought the baby was an attempt to reconcile our differences. But she told everyone the baby was an accident. Then, when Skylar was born with problems…'' He drifted off and stared into the night.

Mallory lightly covered his hand with hers. "I'm sorry, Chase. Really.''

His smile was tight, controlled. He straightened. "There's a better place to talk than here,'' he said suddenly. "You ever hang out in the back of a truck bed and talk about the state of the world today, or tell the ugly parts of your past, and where you want your future to go?''

She shook her head, the hint of a smile on her lips.

"You ought to. It's a Horseshoe Falls kind of thing. Something you ought to acquaint yourself with.'' He reached behind the seat and threw off the top of the cooler he'd packed, pulling out two beers. He handed her one, then hauled out an old tattered blanket and tossed it over the side. "Your carriage awaits, milady,'' he said, going to the back to pull down the tailgate. He offered her a hand up first, and she hoisted herself up. With one hand he shook out the blanket, and Mallory took the other corner to help him spread it out. It fluttered down to the truck bed.

She put a knee down on the blanket, pinning it in place and turned to him. "Okay, this is the hard part for the ribs,'' he said, accepting her hand to crawl up beside her. He groaned from the effort, then lowered himself down beside her, his elbow tucked firmly against his side. They swiveled on their hips and put their shoulder blades against the back of the cab.

The blue-black night enveloped them, and away from the lights of the Haydays celebration, the stars seemed brighter. Chase popped the top on his beer and indicated the unopened can in her hands. "You probably don't even want that."

"It's good to hold when we talk."

He chuckled. "I was telling you about Sharon. Sure you want to hear the rest of it?"

"Yes."

He paused and took a drink. "Sharon yearned for everything I couldn't give her—big-city lights, a hefty bank account, high-class friends—and then, when the baby was born with problems, she was devastated. Skylar, I think, was her compromise to me. And she was a good mom," he added. "She was. But, as parents, we could only make her comfortable. And doing that took its toll." He looked into the distance, remembering. "Skylar was my daughter, no doubt about that. She loved those horses. And she had a real affliction for Peggy Sue."

Mallory tilted her head. "Affliction?" she said carefully, experimenting with her English. "You mean affection. Attraction."

"No, I mean affliction." He chuckled. "She was just taken with that horse. Maybe it was because they were both young, I don't know. But Peggy Sue seemed to just look out for that child, and was actually protective of her, like she sensed Skylar's condition. I'd first named that horse Vanilla, but—and I don't know why—Skylar started calling her Peggy Sue and the name just stuck."

Frowning, Mallory considered this interesting twist. Knowing more about Peggy Sue's history, and how it was intertwined with Chase's life, made things more complicated. Everything in the legend indicated the horse would be more compassionate with a child, particularly an innocent sick child. "So Peggy Sue responded to Skylar?"

"Yeah. If you can call it that. Two-year-olds, especially those with mustang blood, are always a little flighty…but Peggy Sue wasn't nearly as rambunctious when Skylar was around. I'll give her that."

"It's been hard for you, hasn't it, Chase? So much in such a short time."

"It hasn't been a piece of cake, no."

"Cake?" Confusion rolled through Mallory's mind.

Chase laughed, in spite of the delicate revelation. "Another one of those American expressions you hate." He hesitated. "No, there was nothing sweet or easy about it. Bittersweet, maybe. I knew my life was pretty much over with Sharon, even before the baby. But to lose Skylar that way, and so young—" he broke off, his mouth going flat, hard "—I wasn't ready to let her go. None of us were. She made that ranch just sing."

Saying nothing, Mallory gently laid a comforting hand on his leg, just above his knee. "It is hard to watch those we love suffer. I know. I feel the same about my father…and yet, it is different for me. It is always different when a child is suffering, I suppose."

He gave up a small attempt at a smile and nodded. "Everything fell apart after Skylar died. Sharon had spent so much time with her medical care, and she'd spent so much time with the doctor that…she fell in love with him and wanted out of the marriage. It was inevitable, and there was no sense prolonging the pain, not for either of us. So we got a quick divorce. She went on with her life, and I pretty much banished myself to what I had left at the Bar C."

"Banished yourself?"

"Ah, you know. Cut myself off for a while. From

friends, family. Became one of those workaholics everybody talks about. I never patched so much fence or cleaned so many stalls in my life. Sometimes I'd just ride out as far as I could and stay out all night. Pretty selfish of me, really. It was Lewt and Bob who kept things together when I went out of my head like that. They never said nothing, just kept on picking up the slack."

"You are not one to leave things unattended," Mallory said with conviction.

"I did, though. When I lost Skylar, the grief ate me up inside. Divorcing Sharon was just an aftershock. And there was nothing I could do about any of it. I know that now."

Mallory purposely avoided references to Sharon. "Skylar must have been a wonderful, darling little girl."

"She was." He stared thoughtfully into space for a moment, then reached into his back pocket and pulled out his wallet. He flipped through the plastic windows and offered her a glimpse.

By tilting the photo, Mallory could get the reflection off of the corner street lamp. The child, wearing a dark frilly dress, was cherubic, with long, curly blond hair and Chase's teasing grin. "She looks like you," Mallory said without thinking, unaware of the pain that flashed across his features from her comment.

A second elapsed. Then two.

"Mmm. A bit. But I had hopes she'd grow up to be the person—the woman—I've discovered in you. Strong. Kind. Loving. She had those things, her heart just wouldn't let her bring them to adulthood. And the crazy thing about it was that the kid was all heart."

"Perhaps you were a very lucky man, Chase," she said carefully, closing the wallet and offering it back to him. "To have those things in your life, for even such a short time."

"Perhaps. But I'd never ever consider doing it again. I've closed the door and shut the book on that. That part of my life is over. I don't do the involvement and serious relationship stuff. Because I'll never marry or commit myself like that again." He paused. "And maybe that's where you come in, Mallory. There's a part of me that doesn't even want to *like* you. Hell, I shouldn't even be sitting out in this truck with you, looking up at these stars and talking like this, not about my past, not about how I feel—or what I intend to do with the rest of my life."

"What is it you intend to do?" Mallory asked softly.

"Get on with it. Alone."

Then she said the thing she knew he least likely expected, "I understand."

"Do you?"

"We both have other things in our lives. Other commitments. And we'll both see them through," she said earnestly. "I have my family responsibilities. You have your ranch. Our lives have crossed, but they remain worlds apart."

"Literally speaking," he said dryly.

She smiled, sadly, and tucked herself carefully against his side and put her head on his shoulder, knowing full well she shouldn't, knowing she was tempting the course they had each set out for themselves. "It's okay," she whispered softly. "It's enough for us to trust each other, to be friends."

Chase's arms circled her, drawing her comfortably tight. "You know," he said huskily, "if you weren't untouched, a—" he hesitated over the word "—a virgin…I'd take you as my lover."

"I know," she said simply. Then her eyes drifted closed, and she had no alternative but to savor the affectionate kiss he brushed across the top of her head.

They had stayed in the truck until two in the morning. Talking about his life, about hers. She'd told him things she'd never told another person. About how she'd hoped her nanny would fall in love with her father, and they would all run away to the little cottage in the meadow to live happily ever after. Her father would never have to travel on business trips again, and her nanny would grow to love her father's horses and make him proud by becoming a world-famous equestrienne.

Mallory admitted she had even orchestrated situations to put her father and her nanny together. But it had been a dismal failure, all of it. Her nanny detested horses, her father grew impatient when he was away from his business. And then her nanny had the to gall to marry someone twenty years younger than her father and move to England!

That was when she had really begun to study the legends, she said, because they offered the happy endings she sought.

Chase listened patiently, but she knew, intuitively, it was the "happy endings" part he'd heard. Had he offered up even the slightest sign of belief, she might have told him more about what she was thinking. She might have told him all of it.

About Peggy Sue—and about how she suspected Skylar influenced the animal.

As they talked, thoughts of what she'd discovered rolled through Mallory's mind.

Chase's daughter was a child of innocence. Unicorns sought innocence, they recognized it and aligned themselves with it. It was a treasured state, pure and unblemished, and unicorns thrived upon it. It would only make sense that a unicorn would recognize Skylar's purity.

"Chase," she asked suddenly, after Chase mentioned his ex-wife was now happily living in Denver with her new doctor husband, "I thought you said Peggy Sue was gentle with your daughter. What made her change?"

"Neglect," Chase replied bluntly. "It was me. I neglected her in my own grief. I didn't give her the attention she deserved. Because seeing her brought back so many painful memories. I should have made myself keep working with her. I should have done it to honor Skylar's memory." He hesitated. "Now the horse is uncontrollable and I can't bear to let her go. Because it's those same memories of Skylar and Peggy Sue together that bind me to her. No matter what."

"That's why, when I asked to buy her, you refused."

"Partly."

"The other part?"

"I still worry about her harming someone."

"You've seen me with her. You've seen her and what she can do."

He patted his ribs. "Yeah. I know firsthand what she can do."

"You must be serious," she chided. "Peggy Sue has many fine qualities, perhaps you are not yet ready to see and accept them."

"You've brought that horse a long way, Mallory," he said. "Is that what you want to hear?"

Horse? No, the animal was a unicorn—or, at the very least, a portion of unicorn blood ran through her veins. Mallory was convinced of it.

"What I want to hear," Mallory said, "is that you'll do what is best for Peggy Sue. I believe there can be a happy ending for her, and even for the both of us. But I will warn you, it just may not be the ending we would choose."

Chapter Eleven

A week had passed since the Horseshoe Falls Haydays celebration. Chase was getting stronger every day. He still had a few twinges, but that was to be expected.

The real strength, Mallory realized, as she opened the window in her room and prepared for bed, was in their relationship. They laughed easily now, and they relished each other's companionship. Although there were moments they skirted each other like adversaries, Mallory guessed it was because they had revealed too much…and both of them refused to let any physical yearnings complicate what they had planned for the rest of their lives.

Still, it was hard to walk beside Chase and not reach for his hand. It was hard to look up at him and not touch his cheek with her lips for even the most cursory of kisses.

It was strange to have so much driving them apart—even as so much was forcing them together. It was like walking on a ledge, with the winds of change constantly pulling and tugging and pushing at her. She had to keep walking straight ahead, but there were many times she was dearly afraid she'd topple.

She was moving to tame the unicorn, she was moving resolutely forward to fulfill the legend. Yet it was Chase, her stumbling block, who was constantly beside her, who unwittingly encouraged her. Chase Wells was an enigma, and there were times she hardly knew how to separate the man from her mission. There were times she didn't know if she wanted to. He was always with her. His image. His words. His smiles.

He was the first thing she thought of in the morning, he was the last thing she thought of at night.

Mallory untied the belt on her robe and let it slip from her shoulders. She draped it over the chair and turned out the small light on the dresser. The night air was damp and cool, and from the bunkhouse she could hear the faint sound of the radio. One of the cowboys hooted, and she smiled to herself, imagining Lewt was winning at cards again.

When she heard the phone ring, she imagined it was Bob Llewelyn, as he often called at night, to let Chase know what was happening on the road. She turned back the sheets and sat on the edge of the bed, pushing the pillow back against the headboard as she kicked off her slippers.

It would be nice to drift off to sleep, she thought, listening to the quiet murmur of Chase's voice.

Instead she heard his quick footsteps in the hall, then a controlled rap on her door. "Mallory?"

"Yes? Come in." She straightened, pulling herself up from the bed. Before she could turn on the bedside lamp, a shaft of light from the hall illuminated her room.

"You've got a phone call," Chase said, offering her his phone. "From Narwhal."

Mallory hurried from the bed to take the call. "Yes?" she said, omitting the customary greeting.

"Mallory, it's Randolph here."

Randolph LeFavre was her father's personal aid and trusted financial adviser. If there was one man in the world who knew Hewitt Chevalle's business and everyday doings, it was Randolph. "Yes? Randolph?"

"I hate to impose upon your holiday, but I'm afraid it has become necessary."

An ominous premonition welled inside of Mallory, making her stomach lurch. Chase turned to go, to give her privacy with the call, but Mallory's hand shot out to circle his wrist and stop him. "No, it's all right. No bother. I only chose to stay a bit longer. To help out a friend."

She felt Chase's ripple of annoyance. He did not like to be considered an invalid.

"It's your father, Mallory. He didn't want to call you home, but he's taken a turn for the worse. I've taken it upon myself to advise you of his condition."

"Of course. I'd want to know."

"Yes, and Hewitt would call me an alarmist, but…." He trailed off, and it was his silence that worried Mallory even more. "He'd…like to see you, I think."

"Of course. I'll come right home." Mallory hesitated. "How bad is he?" Chase hovered nearer, and Mallory derived undeniable comfort from his closeness, even as she loosed him from her grasp.

"He's experiencing much pain, but his heart is strong and that is the blessing. Perhaps you will be just the tonic he needs. We're hoping for remission, but…it has been this way for many days. Few know, but he has been running the company from his bedside these last weeks."

Mallory's eyes drifted closed. She had called her father frequently, and he'd given her no inkling his illness had progressed. "I had no idea," she said, a guilty note creeping into her voice, "if it weren't for you, looking after him as you do…"

"I am only an extra hand for him," Randolph replied. "Hewitt Chevalle is the cornerstone. This time, I fear, however, that our rock—yours and mine—needs a miracle."

"Oh, Randolph, no…"

"That's why I'm sending a plane for you, my dear. I think you might be that miracle."

Mallory ended the call feeling hopelessly adrift. Narwhal was half a world away. It was too soon to go back, as her plans for Peggy Sue weren't resolved, but she had no choice. "You heard?" she asked Chase.

"I pretty much figured it out, yes."

"My father's health has deteriorated. They need me to come home. Immediately."

"We'll do what we can to make it easy on you, Mallory," he said gently, automatically hooking a finger beneath the spaghetti strap that had drooped over her shoulder, lifting it, then patting it into place. "We can get you into Laramie, or even Denver, and make arrangements from there for a flight."

She flapped her hand. "No. They're sending a plane for me." She missed his surprised look, thinking only of what it would take to make her father heal. She looked up at him. "I'd like to bring Peggy Sue home with me. For my father."

"What?"

"It's her home, Chase," she said earnestly, imploringly. "It's where she belongs."

He snorted, looking over the top of her head and out the window beyond. "You don't give up, do you? You're so determined to have that horse, that even with your father sick and—"

"Chase, no! Listen to me." Mallory twisted off the bed and walked to the other side of the room, nearer the door. "There's something I haven't told you."

He pivoted, following her with his eyes, his features a composite of disbelief. "You ever notice that there's always something you haven't told me?" he asked thoughtfully.

She pulled her robe off the chair and shook it out, unaware that his gaze hungrily claimed her length. "Let's go down and let me fix you a pot of coffee," she offered. "We need to talk about this, and I only have tonight. Tomorrow I have to go home. I'll pack tonight and call Randolph back and arrange for one of our commercial planes and—"

Chase strode across the room to her and jerked her back to face him. "You are assuming I'll let you take Peggy Sue back, aren't you?" he said angrily, his fingers pressing like steel bands around her upper arm. "You can only see what you want! I'd like to know why," he demanded, "that you think that damn horse belongs in Narwhal, like it's her home or her heritage or something."

"I'm convinced it *is* her home," Mallory said evenly. "And she doesn't even know what that means—and, in truth, neither do I. The only thing I know right now is how much it must hurt you, for me to even ask for you to relinquish her." His mouth worked, but he said nothing. "It is a long story, Chase. One that goes back generations. And I have come to believe that Skylar came into her life, for whatever reason, as her caretaker, before she could go home."

His hand fell from her arm. "Every time I think I'm beginning to understand you, you go and say something so outlandish that...I...."

"Let's go downstairs," she suggested softly. "Where we can have a coffeepot and a table between us as we talk."

Chase pulled back and nodded, following her down the stairs.

Mallory couldn't bring herself to look at him, so she just started working on filling the coffeepot, on measuring out the coffee grounds. She kept her back to him and she kept thinking of how much Peggy Sue meant to him. That animal was his last connection to his child.

"Years ago," she began, "before I was born, my family suffered an event that put us at cross-purposes with the legend." Behind her, Mallory heard the legs of a kitchen chair scrape over the tile floor. The wood creaked as Chase sat. "It is why I speak of it so often, I suppose. Because it has affected my family in many ways." She slid the empty coffee carafe on the burner and turned, to choose a chair opposite Chase. "My great-grandfather began the Chevalle shipping empire, but he had a partner. It's said that they fought a lot, but they also made a lot of money." She smiled, thinking of it. "The estate where we now live was my great-grandfather's home and he built it on the thousands of acres that the unicorn were once said to live."

Chase half laughed and shook his head. Mallory ignored him.

"It was my great-grandfather's love of horses that also changed his life," she continued. "He raised some of the world's finest, a breed called the Cornelles, which are now extinct."

Chase's eye narrowed thoughtfully. Brewing coffee gurgled, then trickled into the carafe. "Cornelles," he repeated.

"The Cornelles were alleged to have unicorn blood," she said without wavering. "Their characteristics were similar, but not the same. A white-to-dusky-gray color. A shorter, stockier animal, with large muscle definition. White mane and tail. Silky, not coarse. A small horn—or knotty protrusion on their forehead. Like…Peggy Sue's," she said carefully.

Chase sat back in the chair, considering, his mouth going flat.

"Well, my great-grandfather had the opportunity to bring them to America, to put them on exhibit at a stock show in Denver, and his partner agreed to accompany them. Not unlike the way you and Bob work, I suppose," Mallory commented. "But during his absence, my great-grandfather made a business arrangement that infuriated his partner. He was so angry about it that they dissolved their partnership, and to show his contempt, he took my great-grandfather's prized Cornelles out into the heart of the Rocky Mountains and freed them. It was an act of pure revenge. Of spite."

"No. Wait a minute. There has been nothing but mustangs running through the West for decades," Chase protested.

Mallory smiled. "I know. Efforts were made to recover some of the Chevalle Cornelles, but they were all unsuccessful. It's believed the Cornelles mixed and mingled with the wild horses that ran through the West, diluting their blood even more."

"Let me get this straight. You're saying…?"

"That I hope Peggy Sue has a remnant of Cornelle blood running through her veins."

Chase snorted and his clenched fist thumped the table.

"The family's business foundered for years afterward. Since that event, our family has suffered much personal tragedy, things that the world does not know. Although some old Narwhalians claim that Cornelles still secretly roam the hills of Narwhal, my great-grandfather believed in the prophecy of the legend."

"And that is…?"

"Only the return of the lost unicorn will restore the wellspring of life," Mallory repeated. "That the lost Cornelle must be returned. To my family that means everything. I believe my father could experience relief from the illness that holds him. But he needs to know that the lost Chevalle Cornelle has found its way home."

Chase stood up with a jerk and threw open the cupboard door to grab a coffee mug. He poured himself a cup, then whirled back to face her. "*That* is the tallest tale I think I've ever heard in my whole life. I swear, I've never heard any old cowpoke tell one better. But if you think that some horse with a knot on its head and some little old fairy tale is going to solve your problems, you need to think again." He lifted the cup to his mouth and took a searing drink. "You know what," he said, wincing from the scalding sip, "the only thing running through Peggy Sue's veins is wild, unrestrained anger."

"Peggy Sue related to your daughter because she was innocent and chaste."

Chase stopped and stared at her.

"When did she go crazy with anger?" she asked.

"When I stopped paying attention to her."

"No. When her connection to all that is pure was severed. Unicorns seek that which is chaste and pure and innocent."

"Oh, my—"

"It was never you, Chase! It was something over which you had no control! Can't you see it?" she demanded. "With Skylar gone, Peggy Sue has been lost. It's a grief even she can't control. You had no way of knowing."

"I don't want to—"

"I know," she said quickly. "I didn't want to tell you, either. Not like this. But I didn't randomly come out here to see stock. I came because Bob Llewelyn told me about this horse—a horse with a knot on her forehead, a horse that couldn't be tamed.''

"What do you want?" Chase asked, his eyes shuttering closed.

"Let me buy her from you. Let me take her home to my father. She may not cure him, she may not release my family from the hold the prophecy seems to have on us. But I promise you she will give my father hope. Is that so much to ask? To let my father believe that a horse with Cornelle blood has been found? To merely give him comfort as his illness progresses?"

None too gently, Chase slammed the mug on the counter. Coffee sloshed over the rim. "Let me understand this. No matter what, you're going home to Narwhal."

"I am."

"And you want to buy that blasted horse and pass it off as something with unicorn blood in it."

"Yes…and no. No one needs to know about Peggy Sue. In fact, it would be better if few did."

"The horse isn't for sale, Mallory."

Mallory felt her features go slack and her peripheral vision dim.

"If it means so much to you, I'll give her to you. My parting gift. For your father, and in memory of my daughter, Skylar."

"Chase…thank you. This means the world to me…really…and…"

"Forget it," he groused, "you're the only one who can handle her, anyway. What good is she to me?"

Chapter Twelve

Leaving Horseshoe Falls was the hardest thing Mallory had ever done. She waited until Randolph could arrange the safe transport of Peggy Sue. When she was loaded into her specially made box stall for the trip across the ocean to Narwhal, Mallory turned to Chase. Behind her, the engines thrummed and attendants waited by the plane for her to embark.

"Thank you for everything," she said.

He nodded grimly.

"I'll take good care of her. And I'll see to it she has everything she wants."

He nodded again and looked past her, to the waiting plane.

"I promise you, Chase, that she means everything to me, too. I'll never look at her again without having memories of you. Good memories. Fond memories."

A ripple went down Chase's jaw, and his chin quivered. "You do that," he said huskily, "and you think of me the next time you go up on another Ferris wheel. Remember me as the guy who took you to the top of the world.''

Something behind Mallory's breastbone shuddered, and she choked, half afraid she was going to cry. Instead, she blinked back the red-hot pain behind her eyelids. ''I will,'' she said unsteadily. She couldn't prevent her hand from sliding down his temple and cupping his jaw. ''I wanted to leave you something to remember me by,'' she said softly, ''and the only thing I could think of were those crazy pink cowboy boots you talked me into buying at the Haydays. But I couldn't part with them.'' She rocked back on her heels and let the pointed toes wiggle in his direction.

He choked off a laugh.

''My father would never believe me wearing pink snake-skin boots.''

He started to nod and Mallory acted on impulse to block out the pain she witnessed in the silver depths of his eyes. She leaned forward and grazed his cheek with a kiss. It was only the briefest of farewells...yet it was laden with emotion, because of the bevy of onlookers.

Almost instantly regret mushroomed in Mallory. She imprinted every last detail on her brain: the delectable scent of Chase Wells, the softness of his shirt, the scrape of his beard, the thick bone of his jaw, the hamlike shoulder that shielded her. It was too much to put behind her. Oh, God, she wailed silently, it was too much to lose.

''I—'' she fought to control her quavering voice ''—I've arranged to send you a Narwhal gift package.''

''What? A bottle of wine and a basket of cheese?'' he feebly joked.

''No.'' She couldn't find it in her to laugh. ''A gift from my heart to yours. My favorite mare, Stardust, had her first foal last year. The foal's a beauty with one of the finest bloodlines in the world. A *recognized* bloodline,'' she emphasized. "His name is Galaxy, and I want you to have him. So a part of me will always be with you, too. If he grows into the stallion I think he will, your horses will be world renowned."

"I can't accept—"

"Goodbye, Chase," she said quickly, taking a step back. "I will always—" *love you*, she ached to say "—remember you," she said instead. She moved away from him and experienced a pain so great she thought her heart was being ripped from her body. "You're always welcome in Narwhal. I hope someday you'll let us repay your hospitality." Then she turned and fled up the steps of the waiting plane.

Her father was sicker than Mallory could have imagined. He was sitting in an overstuffed chair when she entered his bedchamber. Although his eyes—dulled by pain and illness—sparked, she could not help but notice his gray pallor, his noticeable weight loss. "You should have told me," she chided, looping her arms around his thin shoulders and kissing his cheek.

He smiled crookedly. "You sounded so happy every time we spoke. I could not bear to take you away from what you'd found on that Wyoming ranch and with that cowboy you spoke so fondly of."

"Oh, Father! The ranch was just a diversion." She shrugged. "The cowboy, just a man." His rheumy eyes narrowed perceptively, making Mallory babble on before she lost her verve. "But it's what I found there," she breathed, her voice thick with undisguised excitement, "and it's what I brought home to you that's important."

"And that would be what? Some silver-studded saddle? Or one of those ten-gallon hats?"

She laughed and went to his wheelchair. "Come along. We're going out to the stable."

He shook his head. "No, it's so wearying to leave my room...."

"What? I can travel all the way from Wyoming, in America, to be with you? And you can't get out to the stables for me, for even a few minutes?" She pushed the wheelchair up beside him. "Indulge me."

"Indulge you?" he grumbled, tossing his lap robe to the side. "You are a spoiled child who pays little heed to the aches and pains of her ailing father."

"Hah!" she retorted, helping him into the chair. "I keep you young."

"So you do, my daughter," he admitted grudgingly, settling into the chair.

Mallory tucked the thick lap robe around him and took the elevator down to the first floor. She could have asked the servants to help her, she supposed, but she wanted to share this moment only with her father, with no mutterings and no *tsking* about what she was doing. They spoke of all that had changed in the weeks since she'd been gone on holiday. She took the back entrance to the stables, and on the way, they both marveled at the herb and vegetable gardens that their cook oversaw.

"Remember the horse show I told you about in California, Father?" she asked quietly.

"Yes?"

"I met a man who spoke of a horse that resembled one of the Cornelles. That is why I went to Wyoming. To find it," she said carefully, easing his wheelchair up to the Dutch doors of the stable. She noticed his hands still on the armrests. She positioned the wheelchair carefully to the side and opened the latch on the top door.

Peggy Sue immediately thrust her head outside, quizzically sniffing the air, before she whickered.

Her father broke into a wide smile.

Mallory lifted the back of her hand to assure Peggy Sue that it was okay, that she was there with her, as she discovered her new home. Chucking her under the chin, she scratched her forehead, then moved her fetlock aside so her father could witness the knobby protrusion.

"Saints be praised," he whispered, his gaze fastened to the stub, "it is true."

"It has taken weeks to gain her trust, but I am convinced she carries the unicorn blood. Her mother fled to the hills and came back in foal, bred by one of the wild mustangs that roam the west."

"A mustang with Cornelle blood," her father agreed, his mind still sharp enough to put the pieces of the puzzle together. He struggled to rise from his wheelchair. Peggy Sue immediately threw her head and went wild-eyed. "Ach, you want the pure of heart," he grumbled knowingly. "You would refuse an old dying man who has searched for you all of his life." Hewitt Chevalle sank back down into his chair with resignation. "And all I want is the feel of your silky mane, the touch of your hide against my hand."

Mallory let go of the halter. "Come here, Father. Lean on my arm and I will hold her so you may have your wish."

He did as she bid him and his spidery fingers flicked over Peggy Sue's neck, then rubbed a strand of her mane between forefinger and thumb. "She must be freed," her father suddenly decreed. "You and I, the last descendants of the Chevalle family, must take her out to the meadow where the unicorn once grazed."

"But...Father—isn't it enough that she is home?"

"No. It must be done before another day shall pass."

"Perhaps, when you're stronger—"

"No, daughter, I will summon the strength for this day. A day long awaited."

Unable to predict what Peggy Sue would do, Mallory fastened the rope lead to her halter and opened the lower door. Her father scuffed back but stayed at Mallory's side. Peggy Sue cooperated, tolerating her father's presence.

They slowly walked to the last gate that was a hundred yards beyond the stable. Her father had left his wheelchair behind and took every step with an agonizing breath. Mallory unlatched the gate, and looked to the thousands of acres of meadow and beyond, to the steep mountains surrounding it. "We may never see her again," she said regretfully.

Her father ran a hand down Peggy Sue's neck and the horse sidestepped away. "Believe, Mallory, that someday those you love will come back to you."

Mallory slipped the halter off of Peggy Sue. The animal bolted away, galloping off into the meadow. Mallory watched her run free, but her mind was on Chase…and the nagging thought that she'd betrayed him.

Hewitt Chevalle experienced relief. It was not the kind that settled into his bones and comforted his aching muscles. It was the kind that made his mind ease. He had left the doors to his balcony open last night. His doctor would chastise him, saying the damp night air was bad for him, yet he needed to let his imagination run as free as the mare he and his daughter had turned out to pasture yesterday.

This morning one of the horses from his stable was kicking up quite a fuss and it annoyed him. Maybe his memories of the Cornelle horse haunted his dreams. Strange that none of the stable boys had seen to it. Throwing back the bedcovers, Hewitt painfully rose from the bed and wandered out onto his open balcony to investigate. There, beyond the gate, the Cornelle Mallory called Peggy Sue whickered impatiently and tossed her head.

"Ach, you are a determined one, eh?" he complained, smiling as he did so. She stamped her foot, and he laughed, seeing the tiny puffs of dirt rise from behind her hooves. He reached for his silk bed jacket and pulled it on, tying the black velvet belt. Glancing over at the wheelchair, he decided against it. A bit more fresh air and some exercise wouldn't hurt.

Hewitt's lungs hurt by the time he reached the mare, but he wouldn't have missed the opportunity to see her one more time. She seemed more tolerant of him this time, even when he reached to rub a curious hand over her horn, something she wouldn't let him close to last night. "Ach, be gone with you and your fussing," he said. "That horn of yours is ivory, sure. With the strength of a unicorn and the heart of a Cornelle. That 'tis what you are, you know."

She shook her head at him, walked a few feet away, then looked back at him.

"What?"

Her look was encouraging.

"You want me to follow you, is that it?" He opened the gate and walked into the great meadow he had not tarried in for years. Oh, it was always the business or the responsibilities. "I'm an old man," he complained. "I can't go far."

Peggy Sue walked a few more steps and paused. Each time Hewitt followed; each time Peggy Sue gave him time to catch his breath. Soon they were a quarter mile away from the stables, near a small cove where he had played as a child. Over the years, the water had gradually disappeared until nothing was left but a dark, damp spot. "I suppose you want a trough here, for water and—" Hewitt broke off, amazed at the sight that spread before him. A spring, with water as clear and clean as a swimming pool, bubbled invitingly. "What the—it's just like when I was a child," he marveled.

Peggy Sue whickered and, with her mane fluttering in the breeze, splashed through the first few feet of water. Then, as the water became deeper, she seemed to dance across the rippling surface.

"I'll be..." Hewitt laughed, then he kicked off his slippers—sickroom slippers, he'd always called them—and dipped his big toe in the water. "It's warm," he chortled, peeling off his robe and his pajamas. "They may think I'm a crazy man, but by God, I'll die a happy one."

The funny thing was, Hewitt reflected later that afternoon, when he'd taken Mallory to the cove to show her, was that he didn't die at all. He'd soaked in those warm springwaters and had emerged with less pain. He was more mobile than he'd been in months.

"You went wading?" Mallory said to her father, looking at him as if he'd lost his mind. "Alone? At five in the morning?"

"The water's warm. Feel it." His voice grew strong with conviction. "Why, there hasn't been water here since I was a child. Then you bring the Cornelle home and—"

"A phenomenon," Mallory dismissed. "Sometimes, every few years—"

"Mallory Leatrice," her father chastised. "You have brought the legend to fulfillment, and yet you remain a doubter?"

"Father, I believe the animal is of unicorn blood. I had many arguments with Chase about it. But this? No. I think that part of the legend is that you want to believe and have healed yourself. The doctors themselves said a remission was possible."

Hewitt Chevalle slanted a narrow gaze at his daughter. "I will come to this spring each morning," he announced, "and I will bathe in the gift you and your friend, this Chase Wells, have given me."

A week later, Mallory was convinced the legend had come to pass. Her father was stronger. He no longer used his wheelchair at all and had tossed several of his pain-killers into the trash. His laugh was hearty and robust and he had begun teasing her about bringing the cowboy, Chase Wells, home for him to meet.

"I want to thank him," her father announced on the tenth day, when he decided to go into the Chevalle shipping offices rather than running things from home. "And someday I shall."

Mallory waved him off to his waiting limousine, fullness welling inside her breast that her father had found some degree of peace. It had been her quest, and she had fulfilled it...but her father could never know what she had traded for his little bit of health. She could never love, not as he imagined a young woman should do. She must keep herself clean and pure of heart, for as long as the Cornelle mare ran in their meadow, Peggy Sue had to know trust and purity rested in their household.

It was a small thing, Mallory reasoned in the lonely weeks that followed, when the servants were busy, her friends were occupied with their families and children and her father was occupied with his business. She tried to think of getting projects together for the summer camps. They were winding down now and it was the perfect time to make plans to expand the riding facilities for next year. But that became tedious.

Instead, she thought of Chase and her darling foal, Galaxy. She wondered if he treasured the foal or ever thought of Mallory.

Mallory saw Peggy Sue every day. She went to the cove daily, looking for her—and Peggy Sue always came, if only for a few minutes.

Mostly, she spent her time imagining Chase's reflection in the water. She imagined his features becoming more weathered, his shirts more worn. While she had grown idle, with a want she could never have, she knew, instinctively, that he worked from sunup to sundown—to banish the pain and the memories.

Peggy Sue came dancing across the waters to her one late August morning. There was a quickness in her step and she was filling out, her coat sleek and soft. "How different you are from those days in Wyoming," Mallory said wondrously.

Peggy Sue tossed her head coquettishly.

"Do you ever think of them? And Chase? And how you seemed to buffalo him?" Mallory could have sworn the unicorn smiled. "I know, I know. Another American expression he taught me." She sighed and watched Peggy Sue cross her front hooves, one over the other as she tripped to the water's edge to pull a few blades of fine green grass into her mouth. "I miss him," she revealed without thinking as she smoothed Peggy Sue's mane. "I really came to care about him. And you know what? Some days I even grieve for his daughter, Skylar, too. Her life was so short…but because of it, I learned about you. If I had known sooner, perhaps you could have helped her, the way you helped my father. That would have been a gift to all of us, wouldn't it? To Chase and me. To give him back everything he gave me."

Peggy Sue's head popped up and she turned around to look at Mallory.

"Oh, I'm just talking. I know it. I just feel somedays like I'm not doing enough for others...and I don't know where to start. It's like something inside me is unsettled. Like you were before you came here."

Peggy Sue swung her rump around and faced Mallory. Then she nudged her. Once. Before she took off.

Mallory stared after her as Peggy Sue climbed up a rocky hillside beside the cove. "Well, I didn't mean to make you mad," she muttered, somewhat annoyed that the unicorn had left her, too.

Ten minutes later, Peggy Sue appeared on the ridge above the cove. She whickered and pawed the ground, sending a tiny shower of stones into the spring. Beside her was a majestic black stallion! He threw his head and reared. When he dropped down beside her, Peggy Sue nuzzled his neck adoringly.

"Why you..." Mallory stopped herself from saying more. "All this time, and you never said a word!"

Peggy Sue and her new friend tossed their heads gaily and were off, a matched pair that literally ran off into the sunset together.

The deepest ache burrowed in beneath Mallory's heart. She longed to run off with Chase, too. To find a cloistered world where love could be shared and honored, where commitment could bind two longing souls.

"Chase Wells," she whispered, "that horse of yours— and that unicorn of mine—is telling me something. Maybe it's time to take you by the shirt collar and shake you up a little. Maybe it's time for me to fashion my own life. To follow—or even create—my own destiny."

Chapter Thirteen

Chase stared out the window at the Atlantic Ocean and wondered what on earth he was doing. He didn't belong on some little itty-bitty island off the coast of France. Not even for a visit. Not even if Mallory Chevalle owned the whole dang thing.

Yet he was going, his hat in his hand—or more succinctly—his hat carefully tucked into the overhead bin. Odd, he'd automatically brought his gray Stetson with him, and then when he'd sat down, he'd wondered why. It would make him stick out like a sore thumb. He should have worn a baseball cap or something.

This whole trip was making him nervous. Probably because she was asking for more than he could promise.

He reached in his coat pocket and fingered the telegram one more time. No need to pull it out. He'd memorized everything it said.

Chase. I need you. Peggy Sue ran away. Searches have turned up little about her escapade. Can you help?

Huh. A telegram. Why didn't she just call? It wouldn't

have hurt one bit for him to have heard her voice. Well…maybe it would have hurt, just a little.

And why send a telegram when she could have sent a plane? As it was, he'd spent two hours at the airport trying to make connections.

Of course, it didn't matter. Not really. He was using this as an excuse to see her again, and he knew it. Sure, he'd stomped around the ranch, bellowing to all the hands that she'd lost that blasted Peggy Sue after all she'd done to locate her and take her home! He'd made enough of a scene that the men had cast him furtive looks. Then he'd caught Lewt mooing like a lovesick calf and Tony patting his heart and rolling his big, brown eyes.

So he'd done the most natural thing in the world. He'd thrown a suitcase together and left. For Narwhal. The mystical, magical island where, according to the travel brochures, it was once purported unicorns thrived and fair, chaste and beautiful maidens lived.

He could endorse at least half that statement—and the other half was grating on him.

After her hasty departure, he'd started thinking of everything Mallory said about unicorns and the legend. She claimed that Peggy Sue had unicorn blood in her veins, and he'd scoffed.

Yet that horse—or whatever—had been attached to Skylar…and that child had been the epitome of innocence.

To be fair, he hadn't neglected that animal any more than the rest of them on the ranch after they lost Skylar. None of the other horses rampaged like Peggy Sue had. He distinctly remembered that her anger erupted the day of Skylar's death. After that it had been a slow, torturous descent. She refused to eat. Her orneriness became just plain mean. Hateful, even. The more he'd tried to control her, the more she fought him. Finally, he had locked her away. The worst thing of all for a unicorn, Mallory claimed.

He thought of that stubby ivory horn on her head. It had grown steadily, until Skylar's death, too. Then it seemed to stop, even shrivel a bit. At the time, he'd been relieved…and the vet had dismissed it as a malformation. But with her temper getting worse, he'd feared it had gone inside—and even though he was sure it hadn't caused her pain, he couldn't say for sure it wasn't affecting her behavior, either. Surgical removal of the horn didn't seem an option. It would be costly, and, the vet had reminded him, she was a half-breed mustang with an attitude.

He shook his head, remembering. He'd done everything to keep her, to gentle her. Yet hadn't he felt relief when she responded to Mallory?

Maybe that was why it had been so easy to give her away like that.

Mallory deserved her. She'd accomplished what he'd never been able to, and he admired her for that. He thought of her suggestion that the horse related to her because she was—*he could barely bring himself to utter the word it seemed so outdated, especially for a healthy twenty-five-year-old woman*—a virgin.

The idea of claiming Mallory's virginity both intrigued and abhorred him. It was like the good and the bad sides of him were battling it out. The good side reminded him he needed to treat her with respect, because she was a lady of virtue, of honor. The other side? Well, hell, that side wanted to toss her in bed and have its way with her. A good healthy roll in the sack, that's what.

But the thing was…you couldn't leave a woman like Mallory, and he knew it. At least he knew he wasn't a strong enough man to leave her, not after that kind of intimacy. Besides, it was one thing to bed a desirable woman—it was quite another to live in bedlam with her. Prior experience confirmed that.

And yet…Mallory wasn't like Sharon. Not at all.

He glanced out the window and caught his breath. There were the magnificent stone cliffs Mallory had described that protected the island on three sides. As the plane drew closer, Chase got a panoramic view of the meadow and the cluster of small towns beyond, to the west. Tiny specks appeared below him. A coiling need stirred in his middle and he wondered, vaguely, if Mallory was one of them.

The realization clutched at him then. He hadn't come to the other side of the world to look for Peggy Sue. He'd come to settle this gut-wrenching turmoil he felt for Mallory.

She invaded his thoughts, constantly. He woke up in the morning and listened for her, disappointed when he came fully awake and realized her absence. So, he'd wind up lying there in bed, reliving the day she'd brought him breakfast on a tray with a single wildflower. He'd go downstairs, fighting mad and aching to clear his head, get back on track and suck up a cup of coffee—only to reminisce about the coffee Mallory had once fixed.

All his days were like that. Everywhere he went, there was some blasted, taunting, bittersweet recollection of Mallory. An in-your-face kind of reminder.

The currycomb Mallory had used on Peggy Sue. The spot she'd hung over the corral fence. The pickup, where she'd once hung her elbow out the window and finger-combed her hair at her temple back to gaze at him.

He'd never been one to understand that old phrase, "wearing your heart on your sleeve," but he understood it now. He looked down now and stared at the cuffs of his western shirt, wondering if this crazy, insane way he'd come to care for her showed.

She *had* affected him, he couldn't deny that.

But it was a residual effect. Leftover feelings, leftover memories. Some needed clarification; some just needed to be put to rest.

Closure. That's what this trip was about.

Maybe he should have warned her he was coming, he thought ruefully as the plane began its final descent, because he didn't quite know what he was going to find or how things were going to turn out.

Otswego, the capital of Narwhal, was a quaint bustling community. Two-story homes, painted in arresting hues of green and blue, capped with red-tile roofs, lined the cobblestone streets, town-house fashion. Every window facing the street had a window box stuffed with brilliant flowers. Street corners boasted fancy sculptures or magnificent statues. Chase craned his head out the window of the taxi, to inhale more of the sweet, fresh fragrances, to absorb more of the eclectic charm that was Narwhal.

Time warp, Chase thought absently, taking in the curious mixture of men wearing business suits, Italian shoes and the *troinoux,* a dark tricorner hat, favored by Narwhalians. Laborers all wore the same black boots and shapeless brown pants. They passed a huge stone fountain, where toddlers played beneath the watchful eye of their mothers— and Chase wondered if Mallory had ever been allowed to play in the public fountains. Probably not. She was the revered daughter of Narwhal's wealthiest citizen.

The taxi driver pulled up in front of the Chevalle estate, and Chase caught his breath. The grounds were surrounded by a tall iron fence, and behind, the house sprawled—a storybook castle—with turrets, balconies, and parapets. The taxi driver asked for two *fasoux*—barely five dollars American money—and Chase, unable to tear his gaze from the estate, fumbled to get it out of his wallet.

He learned from the get-go, however, that men wearing cowboy hats, boots and jeans do not just go up and walk through the front gate of the Chevalle estate. He was immediately stopped by two uniformed guards sporting billy clubs, mace and snub-nosed revolvers; their dogs were tethered by leather leashes. No way was he going to try to outrun any of them.

He waved the Western Union telegram at them. "I'm here to see Mallory Chevalle. She asked me to come."

The fairy-tale atmosphere immediately evaporated. Both guards sneered, then laughed. "Mallory Leatrice Chevalle does not invite men to the estate," the older man announced, in heavily accented Narwhalian.

"Yeah? Well, she invited me," Chase said, pushing the telegram at him.

The guard studied the paper, then motioned his counterpart to the phone. Apparently the Chevalle hotline. "Please sit," the guard directed.

Chase did as he was told, but an uneasy feeling washed over him. He had no idea this was how Mallory lived, like a prisoner in some ivory tower. He'd never be able to do it, not for one minute.

Maybe that was why she'd cherished her freedom in the United States, maybe it was that, and it wasn't him at all. Maybe he'd overestimated their little—what?—fling. Maybe that's why he hadn't heard from her in all these weeks, and she only needed him now for his expertise.

Crud, look what she'd done to him. She had him second-guessing everything. She had him wondering and riddled with indecision.

No woman was worth that, he reminded himself fiercely.

He'd get that damn Peggy Sue back for her and then he
was done. He was out of here. He was history.

"Sir? My apologies for detaining you. Perhaps you
would like some tea while you wait? We have a fine Narwhalian blend, with mint."

Chase's jaw slid off center. Their attitudes, and that of
their guard dogs, had visibly changed. "Nah, that's okay,
I'll just mosey on inside, if that's okay."

"Mosey?"

It struck Chase then how he was always explaining his
pet phrases to Mallory, too. It had been one of the most
endearing facets of their time together. He lifted a shoulder.
"I'll just go on in," he said, biting back a grin.

"I'm sorry, sir. A car has been assigned to pick you up."

Chase couldn't contain his amazement. "But I can see
the place from here!" In seconds, a flashy red convertible
careened down the drive, between the exquisitely manicured flower beds. Chase's insides turned to mush when he
saw the familiar halo of blond hair, the distinctive tilt of
her head.

Mallory was behind the wheel, and she came to a
screeching halt, jumped out of the car and waved. "Chase!
You came! I wasn't sure if you would!"

He moved toward her as if he was on autopilot.

She flung herself into his arms, and he noted that she
was deliciously animated, her cheeks pink, her hair more
sun-streaked than he remembered. "I've missed you," she
said, giving him a tight squeeze, "so much."

The impact of her body against his, he conceded irra-
tionally, was even better than when his arms were full of
her at the street dance. He hugged her back, inhaling her
fragrance. She had only grown softer, her breasts flattening
against his chest in an accommodating sort of way.

Time had only made things better.

Just as quickly, she jerked away. "Oh! Your ribs. Are they okay? Are you better?"

"Never better," he said huskily.

She ran both hands down his sides, in a cursory examination over his blue shirt. "We spent so many nights together, trying to get it right," she said. "And every so often you'd cry out. I was always afraid I'd hurt you."

He knew she meant the gauze bandages. But, from his peripheral vision, he saw the guards exchange wide-eyed glances, and promptly shut his mouth to avoid any explanation. It would only embarrass her. "Guess I ought to learn to grit my teeth a little more, Mallory," he said, chuckling.

She smiled up at him, a dazzling, for-your-eyes-only kind of smile.

Warmth suffused him, and suddenly he was glad he hadn't bought the return ticket. "Be careful. You keep smilin' at me like that, darlin', and I may never go home."

Her smile widened. "Good. Because I have much to show you."

"And Peggy Sue?" he asked. "I suppose she's still on the loose? No word there?"

Mallory immediately sobered. "Well…yes. But we can talk about her later," she quickly dismissed. "Have you met Roderick and Claude?"

Chase tipped his head. "Fellows."

"Sir," they both intoned.

"They'll see to it that you aren't stopped again, and that you can come and go as you please," Mallory said. "I know you aren't used to this kind of thing. But my father insists."

"Smart man. Not to let anything happen to you."

She bestowed a fond gaze his direction, and later he realized her response was cryptic. "But things do happen,

Chase. A lot has been happening to me. I've learned there are some things in life you just can't prevent. And sometimes you just don't want to."

"I'm sorry to keep you waiting," Mallory said, joining him on the patio a short time later.

She'd said she wanted to change, but the last thing Chase expected was a stunning backless sundress that tied at the nape. Never having seen her in a dress before, he gaped. Then, immediately minding his manners, he stood, waiting until she was seated to put a hand on the back of her chair. He unintentionally brushed her bare shoulder and jerked back, guiltily, as a ping of electricity went through him.

This was a different woman from the one he had come to know on the Bar C. This woman was polished and cultured and accepted her opulent lifestyle as if it were ordinary.

He glanced uncertainly from Mallory, down to the spread in front of him. It was definitely not macaroni and cheese, or meat loaf.

"You haven't eaten," she said, a hint of disappointment in her voice. "I thought you'd be famished."

"I—" he lifted a shoulder "—wanted to wait for you." The truth was he hadn't wanted to make a mess out of the fancy arrangements by digging in. Every sauce was drizzled artistically, every raw vegetable was fashioned in some kind of little curlicue.

"You don't like anything," she said flatly, surveying the platters and plates.

"No, no," he said quickly. "It's…nice." Mallory blanched at his poor choice of words. "I just thought we'd share. You know, eat together."

"Cook likes to go overboard. We indulge her because she's so proud of her work. But I'm sure she's showing off for you. Really. The upstairs maid mentioned that Claude made a big deal out of me having a gentleman guest.''

"You make it sound like that's an unusual occurrence."

Mallory laughed. "It is. I do believe the staff has taken wagers on whether I shall require the services of a match-maker or simply become an old maid."

"You can't be serious. You? An old maid? Never."

Mallory shrugged, then poised her fork over the cheese-and-chive potatoes. She scooped up a generous amount and offered him a taste. Never taking his eyes off of her, he nibbled a bit from the tines of her fork.

"Delicious."

"Mmm, and now we've shared the same fork and given the staff something to gossip about," she teased. "Not un-like Lewt and Tony and Gabe, I suppose. People are the same the world over. Whether in Narwhal or America." She popped the remainder of potato into her mouth, and Chase watched in fascination. She made everything seem so easy. Even the differences in their stations.

"Are your rooms all right?" she continued, offering him the lemon-flavored white fish.

"Yes. Fine." He concentrated on the entrée, but the bottom line was that everything around him was so formal, he felt like a fish out of water—like the one that was being served up on a silver platter.

His room had been hung with tapestries and gilt mirrors, for cryin' out loud. His bed was so high, there was a step stool beside it. He would have been more comfortable with a bedroll out at the stable, but he couldn't come out and say that. "You haven't told me about your father. Or your work with the children's summer camps."

Mallory hesitated. "My work. There is much to do. I hope to build another arena this winter, but…"

"Yes?"

"I've found that the things I used to do alone no longer bring me the same kind of joy. I miss being with you and Lewt and Tony and Gabe on the ranch." Heat radiated from the center of Chase's breastbone, and he warmed. "I liked the way everyone worked together. I find…my days alone, now that my father is well, do not bring me the same satisfaction."

Chase stared at his glass of wine, wondering if she could possibly have missed him as much as he'd missed her. "So," he said finally, avoiding her references to her time in Wyoming with him on the ranch, "your father is better."

She nodded. "He is well. Better than he has been in years."

"He liked Peggy Sue, then? Having her around lifted his spirits?"

Mallory contemplated her answer, slowly filling her luncheon plate with a variety of fruits and salads. "When I arrived home, Chase, my father was nearly bedridden. His strength was gone. He hadn't been to his offices in weeks." She carefully put the serving spoon back in the bowl. "He believes Peggy Sue has special talents, Chase. Because of that, he and Peggy Sue have a bond that is uncommon."

"Like Skylar and Peggy Sue?"

"Perhaps. But for different reasons, I think. Peggy Sue recognized my father's illness. She also recognized that this was her home. She *knew* that, Chase. From the beginning." She paused, seeing the skepticism in his eyes. "I wish I could convince you of that."

Chase pushed some of the food around on his plate. "I'm not here to argue about it," he said quietly, "so let's just leave it at that. But your father? Did he see the same things in her you did?"

"My father firmly believes she is a descendant of the

Cornelles,'' she replied. ''And in her own way, she has offered up proof of her lineage.''

Chase raised a quizzical brow. ''You can't be serious.''

''After luncheon, I will show you.''

''But you don't know where she is?''

Mallory offered him her sly Mona Lisa smile. ''She is somewhere on the island, Chase. We do know that.''

Chapter Fourteen

Mallory took Chase to the stables to show him some of their stock. He was duly impressed. She pointed out Peggy Sue's designated stall, but warned him the animal had only spent a few hours there. "My father was adamant that she be put out to pasture that first night. That was, he said, where she deserved to be."

"So you just let her loose, and she ran off. Is that it?"

She scuffed at a pebble with the toe of her shoe and avoided his look. "No. Not exactly. There is more to it than that."

"Why don't you just whistle and she'll come back. Like you did on the ranch."

She laughed. "You give me too much credit."

"No, I don't think so. I saw it happen with my own eyes."

She shrugged. "I think," she confided, leaning against his shoulder, "that right now Peggy Sue is ignoring me. She has made a decision to follow her heart, instead of listening with her head."

"I'm disappointed in you," he said, grinning. "I thought you had her trained."

"Ah. As if you have never wanted to follow your heart," she retorted, leading him away from the stable. "You and I, we have spent our life thinking things through and deciding what path we will follow."

"Is that so wrong?"

Mallory didn't answer. "Peggy Sue, she moves like a spirit now, wherever her feet—or the wind or the scent of new grass—urge her to go. In her, I see a freedom I have come to envy."

He slowed, considering. "You say that as if something has been lacking in your life." He took in the mansion and manicured yard, the stables, the tennis court and pool.

She followed his gaze, but it was her silence that reminded him some things were not attained with money.

They walked together to the gate and looked across the unfenced meadow. "This is some pasture," Chase approved. "I can picture you, Mallory, riding here. I can imagine Galaxy here."

She turned to him. "How is he?" she asked eagerly.

"Remarkable. People have come from all over the country to get a glimpse of him."

She smiled. "I'm glad."

"He's more than I deserve, Mallory. I've thought many times he should be returned here, to his roots…but, Bob—well, hey, I've got to admit you'd need to pry him loose from Bob's hands."

She laughed, obviously pleased. "If Galaxy's content, that is my only concern. I consider him Bar C stock now. He is only a small token of appreciation for all you've given me. Come on," she invited, changing the subject and throwing back the gate. "There will be time for us to ride together later, and for me to show you some of my favorite places. Now there is something else I want to show you."

She steered him toward the cove, but his eyes were riveted on the surrounding mountains, the steep white cliffs. She knew he was thinking of the legend, she could see it in his eyes. "Are you looking for Peggy Sue?" she asked.

"What else? I get the strangest feeling she's watching us."

Mallory linked her arm through his. "She probably is," she said.

They turned beyond some linden trees and he stopped, obviously surprised at how quickly they were swallowed up in the privacy of the secluded glen. A profusion of ferns and delicate white flowers clustered in the background, and thick hanging vines offered a dense screen. "My father," she said, "used to play here when he was a child. But for as long as I remember, this place was only a damp spot on the ground. Now look at it."

Chase stood stock still, staring at the clear blue water, the lush foliage, the outcropping of rock and the stepping-stones. "This is like something out of the movies." He moved forward, then knelt on a small flat rock that jutted over the water and dipped his hand into it. "It's warm as bathwater," he exclaimed, looking over his shoulder at her.

"My father says it has therapeutic value."

He pulled back, frowning. "Now…wait a minute. Don't tell me this is the Fountain of Youth or something." She laughed. "I mean it, what with all your talk about legends and unicorns and things, I don't need to hear something like that."

"You have mineral baths in America," she pointed out. "I've been to them."

His jaw worked. "That's different," he finally muttered. "They're left over from a different era."

She smiled, refusing to argue. "The first night we brought Peggy Sue home, we freed her, Chase. And the next morning, she came back and led my father to this spring. It appeared as if by magic. Every day for two weeks, Peggy Sue came for him early in the morning and he swam here. Every day he grew stronger." She moved behind him and kicked off her shoes. Then she sat beside him as he still balanced on his haunches, and she pulled her skirt up above her knees to dangle her feet in the water. "I think it is a strange coincidence to have so many things happen at once, yes?"

"Mallory..." He couldn't help it. His attention was drawn to her long, slim legs. To the curve of her calf, and the scintillating water that speckled her ankle and shin. She was so incredibly beautiful.

"Think of it, Chase. My father has been sick for years. And I have sought to fulfill the prophecy of the legend for just as long. I came to Wyoming, searching for the Cornelle. And Peggy Sue related to me, and to my—" she looked away, shyly, into the depths of the rippling water "—innocence. Just like she did to Skylar's."

Chase stared through the water, at ten berry-painted toenails.

"And when I brought her home," Mallory continued, "the spring appeared." She paused. "In the legend, it is called the wellspring of life."

"Mallory..."

"And yet my father grows stronger," she reminded.

"No. Things happen. Strange things. Things that can never be explained."

She smiled sympathetically, then gently touched his knee and leaned into his thigh. "Is that," she whispered, "what they call a prophecy?"

"I like your first suggestion of coincidence better. It's something we can agree on."

"All right," she laughed, "I will accept that. For now." She dragged her toes over the water, creating a small wake. "I swim here, too, you know."

"Really? Even when you've got that nice big chlorinated pool up at the house?"

"Mmm, yes. This is so peaceful, so comforting." She moved away from him slightly, putting her shoulder parallel with his. "I came here at first to look for Peggy Sue. Then later, when I thought about you and how far away Wyoming was. Especially that. Sometimes, when I was here, I reminded myself Wyoming was on the other side of the world."

He hesitated for a mere fraction of a second. "Did you miss me, Mallory?" He held his breath after asking the question, half afraid of what the answer would be.

"Of course," she said easily. She turned her head, gazing up at him with the most hopeful expression.

She wanted him to say that he'd missed her, too. He could see it in her eyes.

He had—he'd missed her terribly—yet the acknowledgment seemed to stick on his tongue. "I, um—" he looked away "—well, I figured you'd be too busy getting back to your old life. Looking after your father, your business interests, your horses."

"I'd never be too busy to forget people who are important to me, Chase," she said softly. "And you? You're important to me. We made a lot of good memories back in Wyoming. We shared a lot of secrets when we were in the back of your truck, looking up at the stars. I don't think I've ever been so close to another person. Not in my whole life."

Chase winced, vividly remembering all he'd told her

about losing his daughter, and the messy dissolution of his ill-fated marriage. "Sometimes getting too close brings out the hurtful side of a person, Mallory."

"I thought getting close brought a lot of comfort for all that hurt. It did for me. I discovered a tender, bruised heart inside of you. After that night, I thought it was just aching to heal again. Tell me," she said, "was I wrong?"

He gnawed indecisively on his lower lip, thinking of all the things he had bottled upside himself for so very, very long. Mallory probed into his deepest feelings, without making him feel threatened or vulnerable or weak. She had a knack for making him smile again, of winning him over with her strength, her patience and determination. She was one extraordinary woman, and he was a better man for having her pass through his life.

"Come on," Mallory said abruptly, unfastening her skirt. "Since you aren't going to answer me, we can go skinny-dipping, like Lewt says you do in Wyoming. That would be fun. And it won't be so serious."

Chase pulled back, his head reeling with this new, confusing twist. "Mallory! What are you doing?"

"I'm going swimming. With you," she stated matter-of-factly.

"Oh, no! Wait a minute! If your father finds us, like this...or those two guard guys at the front...why they'd string me up and..."

Mallory grinned, then pulled the skirt off her lap, briefly revealing a sexy two-piece swimsuit. A curling sensation gripped his loins.

She slid off the rock and water lapped at her waist. "Come on," she cajoled. "You know you want to."

"I came out here to look for that horse," he argued, straightening to stand.

"Well, you can if you want to...but—" she shrugged "—I think I'll just cool off first."

Chase looked down at her—straight down into the cleft of her swimsuit, to the dark, luscious hollow, and to her firm, swollen breasts. Duty and desire came to an impasse.

"There's a spot over there where you can put your jeans and your boots," she suggested mildly. "Go ahead. I'll turn my back." She swam away, to the deeper part of the pool.

Chase stared after her and wondered what the hell he was going to do. The surrounding water didn't just distort her physical body, it enhanced it, making it more provocative than anything should have a right to be.

He shouldn't feel this way for her. It wasn't fair to her. She deserved better. She deserved a first-time go-round with a man who believed in marriage and commitment and kids.

He took two steps back, intending to get as far away from her as he could possibly get—and promptly lost his balance. He fell flat on his back, straight into the warm, waiting water.

A vortex of sensation swirled around him. The pressure of water gripped him, lifted him. It rushed in his ears. It tasted like a healing tonic on his tongue. The heat soothed him like a balm. The comforts the pool unexpectedly offered up were brief, and yet they lasted forever.

The wellspring of life, he thought absurdly, still submerged.

An intense relief, akin to a complete cleansing, relaxed his limbs. His head cleared and pain floated away. His roiling stomach soothed.

Perhaps this pool did have healing powers, he allowed.

As his physical body floated to the surface, the past faded into another, absent lifetime. An incredible feeling of hope welled within his breast. Visions of the future he could create—of the love he could share—flitted behind his eyelids.

Destiny had always seemed to play a part in his life, and when he opened his eyes, his vision fell directly on Mallory. She had the most angelic smile on her face, the most serene light in her eyes. Water shimmered around her, like a halo rippling before it slowly radiated outward.

He was mesmerized; he couldn't drag his gaze away.

"You decided to join me," she said.

He blinked. "Yeah. I guess I did."

He was vaguely aware that, beside him, his hat bobbed on the water.

"How's the water?"

"It feels…" He was at a loss for words. He could think only of her, and how she affected him.

"Yes?"

"Soothing. Like a lot of my troubles have been washed away."

"Ah, they probably have. As for myself, I found a tranquillity here—and it helped me know what I wanted."

He stared at her. Hard. Knowing for the first time in a long time what he really wanted in life. He wanted to share his life again, with a woman like Mallory.

No. *With* Mallory. Specifically Mallory.

Mallory cupped her hands, letting water trickle between her fingers. "How about if we take a swim and you can enjoy the benefits of this special pool."

"Actually, I think I already have," he said, unsnapping his shirt and peeling it off. Flinging his sodden shirt on the outcropping of rock, he leaned down to pull off his boots. Before setting the first on top of the ledge, he poured out the water.

Mallory laughed.

He did the same with the second. Then he moved toward

her and started unbuckling his belt. He detected the slightest flush of anticipation in her cheeks, and the involuntary gesture endeared her to him.

She was so intoxicatingly beautiful, and he consciously memorized every detail, every nuance of her reaction.

He worked the copper button on his jeans through the buttonhole, and saw that her eyelashes fluttered. When he unzipped his jeans and pushed the waistband down, her lower lip trembled.

Finally, he kicked his way out of the denim, and he was rewarded to see the corners of her mouth curve.

He slung the whole wet mess beside the shirt, then he ran a thumb beneath the elastic waist of his briefs. "You sure you want to do this skinny-dippin' thing?" he teased. "It means getting bare-butt naked."

Mallory spread her arms, fanning them over the surface, and trailed her fingertips through the water. "What will it matter? We have all this water between us."

He chuckled but didn't make a move. He felt more alive than he had in a decade. His heart felt about to burst. Love, passion, desire, it was all there, wrapped up in one neat little package—and it all hinged on one thing: Mallory.

Mallory tipped her head forward and lifted her arms, to her nape, where the wet ties dangled down her back. In the chest-high water, she slowly worked the knot. The neckline buckled, then one side of her suit sagged.

Chase caught his breath, transfixed.

Mallory drew the front of her suit across her chest, revealing only the full tops of her breasts. The rest of her, naked to the waist, was left to Chase's vivid imagination. "It feels," she said carefully, "like this is the Garden of Eden, certainly not the Fountain of Youth."

He watched her carefully pair her hands at either side of her waist, and push down the small, tight shorts. Everything in him tensed. His heart rate accelerated, his blood tremored. His mind hummed with possibilities.

He had never before known a woman who so forthrightly offered herself up with such courage and innocence. It was an irresistible combination, and he was losing his heart to it.

"Mallory…?"

"Yes?"

"I came to Narwhal because I wanted to. Because of you." *There.* He'd said it. Without compunction or fear or regrets. "Because I couldn't stop thinking of the difference you'd made in my life."

"We complement each other, Chase."

"I didn't come because of Peggy Sue."

Mallory's expression grew serious, thoughtful. "I wasn't completely honest. I didn't invite you here because of Peggy Sue, either. I invited you here because of me."

A slow, dawning smile eased onto his features.

She returned his smile, then the shorts appeared in her hand and floated briefly on the top of the water before sinking to the bottom of the pool in a muted flash of color. "I needed to see you again and make a few memories with you here, on 'my stomping ground,' as you like to say."

Chase chuckled and pushed the elastic down over his hard, teeming flesh, to step out of his briefs. Frankly, he didn't care if he ever recovered them…they could stay lost at the bottom of this incredible pool. Being with Mallory was the only thing that mattered.

He swam to her side, then stopped suddenly. God Almighty, what was he supposed to do with a virgin who was naked as a jaybird and only three feet away?

He wanted to tell her he loved her. Hell, he wanted to shout it from the top of the world. From one side of this magnificent glen to the other!

As if she picked up on his exuberance, his joy, Mallory laughed and swam just out of his reach.

"Not fair!" he retorted, catching her ankle.

She squealed and twisted away.

She splashed him; he splashed back. She did a surface dive to escape, and he followed, letting the deep shadows of the pool cover their nakedness. Together they reached for each other and joined hands, swimming underwater toward some unknown destination. Their bodies, clothed in the murky waters of the deep, sleekly became one, side by side.

They surfaced together, their clasped hands raised.

Mallory's hair was slicked back from her face. Her wet spiky lashes were a shade darker. The most delectable droplet of water wobbled invitingly on her lower lip.

"I never got to kiss you hello," Chase said huskily, positioning himself in front of her.

"And that kiss goodbye, when I left Wyoming, didn't really count," Mallory replied, gazing up at him.

They moved together as if the moment were preordained, and nothing could have prevented it. Water surged between them, then receded. All resistance faded away...into acceptance, and a joining of their hearts.

Yet when they actually, physically, touched and his chest brushed against her swollen breasts, Chase hesitated.

Mallory's eyes went dark and heavy-lidded. "We were just as close when we danced in the street," she reminded silkily.

"But..."

She inched closer to him, looping her arms around his neck, to draw him down for a kiss. Her curves fit against his, accommodating his hardening planes. Chase did the most natural thing in the world, he gathered her up to him, against his heart, and he claimed her lips.

Their magical, mystical world spun out of control, nothing but heady sensation existed. Colors blurred, the water warmed to a new heated temperature. The sandy bottom of the pool sucked them down, holding them firmly in place, weighting their every move.

Chase succumbed to the druggedlike state, cherishing it. He pulled away, brushing another kiss across her cheek, the shell of her ear. "Back in Wyoming, I convinced myself I was coming to find Peggy Sue, but in my heart I knew I had to find you instead," he whispered. "I couldn't let you go. Not in my head. Not in my heart." He felt her tremble in his arms. "I love you, Mallory. I think I fell in love with you from the first moment you stepped out of that flashy convertible."

"Really? It took you *that* long?"

He grinned, remembering. "You looked just like this angel coming into my life, stepping right out and intending to set things straight."

"Someone needs to set you straight, Chase Wells. And, as for me, I love you enough to do it."

"Do you? Do you really?"

"I think of you, Chase, and sometimes my heart just hurts from loving you so much. I've been doing a lot of hurting, too, these past months without you."

They appraised each other, realizing they had just opened their hearts for scrutiny, for rejection, for the ultimate reckoning only two people can offer up...all in the name of love. They shared, for the briefest moment, a for-your-eyes only exchange.

Chase looked deep into Mallory's clear blue gaze and found the woman of his dreams.

Mallory looked into Chase's dark, perceptive gaze and saw the man she idealized.

"I love the way you laugh," he said. "The way you joke about things."

"And, me? I love the way you try to act tough and strong. Everyone knows you are just a pussycat underneath."

"A pussycat?" He pulled back slightly, feigning indignation.

"You are soft, in all the ways that count most to a woman."

"Soft?"

"Ever so soft when you say you love me." She tilted her head. "Say it again. Please."

"I love you, Mallory Chevalle of Narwhal. And," he added more loudly, "I don't care who knows it!"

A whicker of appreciation sounded, and both Chase and Mallory startled. They looked up, overhead, to the source. Standing proudly on the ledge high above them was Peggy Sue. Her ivory horn was completely visible through her fetlock, and she was no longer gaunt, but perfectly sculpted with a visceral beauty. Her sleek mane and tail, riffled by the light breeze, created a dreamy illusion.

Chase and Mallory imperceptibly pulled apart. "I've never seen anything like that," Chase murmured. "She's incredible."

Peggy Sue swung her great head back, over her shoulder, then paused before she nimbly picked her way down the slope. She disappeared from view, and for a moment, Chase experienced the fleeting fear that he'd never see her again.

When she reappeared, both Mallory and Chase turned to face her. Peggy Sue picked her way around the pool, coming to stand on the outcropping of rock, where he'd flung his wet clothes.

"Go on," Mallory urged him. "She's come to see you."

Chase eased forward, filled with disbelief that this was

the same animal he'd sent home with Mallory. He stood before her in the waist-high water and extended his hand.

Peggy Sue, true to form, ignored it. But she leaned closer, sniffing, to nuzzle the side of his face, his neck. She whickered softly, then gave him butterfly kisses with the velvety tip of her nose.

He heard Mallory come up to stand behind him at his side.

"Her horn is longer," he said.

"Mmm."

"And she seems gentler."

"Mmm, yes. I'd say so."

"What's come over her?" he asked incredulously.

Peggy Sue lifted an eyebrow, as if she found his questions amusing. She looked over at Mallory and shook her head, as if they were sharing a private, female joke.

"Peggy Sue's a happy little lady now," Mallory said, "since she's found her soul mate."

"Her...what?"

As if he heard his calling, the exquisite black stallion Mallory had come to expect at Peggy Sue's side appeared. He reared on the precipice of the ledge and sent a small shower of gravel skittering into the pool. Then he pawed the ground and whirled, and rampaged down the side of the hill.

"Well, well, well. I see she's met her match," Chase said dryly.

The stallion skidded to a stop, fidgeting on the other side of the pool as he waited for her to join him. Peggy Sue's head shot up, and she eyed him lovingly. She cast Chase a benevolent look, then leisurely strolled around, in the wide circle created by the pool, to her mate.

Chase watched her go. "Okay, Peggy Sue," he said softly. "You've convinced me you're home. You've pretty much convinced me you're a unicorn, too. I'll grant you that. But I'd do just about anything to see you walk on water.''

Peggy Sue stopped short and her right ear flipped back. She paused momentarily, then she swung her great head around to quizzically appraise him.

''Um…Chase…'' Mallory intervened. ''You better be careful what you promise.''

''What?'' he asked in surprise. ''Like it's going to happen and she's going to hold me to it?''

Peggy Sue's ears went flat, and she fixed him with a no-nonsense stare.

Mallory jumped into the fray. ''She wants you to promise to go on with your life,'' she said. ''Just like she's going on with hers.''

Chase frowned at Mallory, then he whirled back and his gaze collided with Peggy Sue's.

Just as quickly, she snorted and tossed her head. Her tail flicked across her hips and her feet seemed to trip on thin air. Then she took off, dancing across the water as if it were a shimmering glass plate. When she reached the deepest part of the pool, she reared on her hind legs and executed an astonishing pirouette. Then she scampered across the surface of the water to the other side, and to the approval of her mate.

''Well, I've never seen *that* before,'' Mallory said.

Chase said nothing, but he had the most confounded expression on his face. He watched the unicorns run into the meadow and disappear from view. Finally, he reached for his still wet shirt and pulled it off the ledge and into the pool. ''I'll be damned. And I promised her,'' he said, almost to himself.

''Yes?''

''To go on with my life.''

"I know, Chase. But…you don't have to go out and do anything drastic."

"Oh, no, this time around I know what I want and I know where I'm going," he said decisively, shaking out the shirt. "But no more skinny-dipping."

Trepidation magnified in Mallory. Was he angry? Did he feel he'd been deceived?

Chase gave the shirt a good flap, then swung it around and draped it over her shoulders.

The gesture left Mallory suddenly, and uncomfortably, aware of her nakedness. She had come remarkably close to surrendering her virginity this afternoon. How humiliating to have him reject her now. "What are you doing?" she said shakily, clutching the ends of the sodden shirt to her breast.

"First off," he announced, grabbing his hat as it floated alongside him, "I'm going to do the right thing and make an honest woman of you. I want to feed you toast in the mornings and share your pillow at night."

She jerked, uncertain she heard him properly. "You're going to do…*what with my pillow?*" She stared at him, physically feeling her pupils dilate and her eyelids widen. "These are more American sayings, yes? Jokes, yes?"

He chuckled, and his mouth slid into the most irresistible lopsided cowboy grin. "No, it's not a joke at all." He swept her with a penetrating gaze, then pulled his wet hat to his chest. "I'm coming with my hat in my hand, Mallory. Will you marry me? Will you have me? We shouldn't be here, skinny-dippin' in a pool, not without the benefit of a marriage. We need to be together, and we need our names side by side on a marriage certificate. I love you. Will you marry me?"

Her knees went weak, but behind her breastbone her heart thrummed. Never in a million years, or a dozen unicorn prophecies, would she have imagined this. *Say yes, say yes, say yes,* her subconscious urged. "But—but…when?" she said instead.

His eyes lingered at the top of her wet head, then raked her shoulders, her front. The knuckles on his hands went white as he mashed the hat against his body. "As soon as possible," he said hoarsely. "Because I can't wait that much longer. I honest to goodness can't. We have reasons to be together and I think we ought to honor them."

Chapter Fifteen

They had done everything the traditional way. Chase had formally asked Mallory's father for her hand in marriage, and he had happily given it. For ten days Mallory replayed the scene over and over again in her head.

"It is as if the fates have spoken and blessed this union," Hewitt Chevalle had announced grandly, insisting that his finest bottles of wine grace the table for the occasion. "I trust it is part of the prophecy, that my beloved daughter will marry and share an eternal love."

The plans for the wedding, and for their life afterward, went rolling along.

"I've got it all worked out," Chase announced, striding into the drawing room. "Just like we discussed."

"Chase!" Mallory reproved. "You shouldn't be in here. I'm making decisions on my trousseau!"

He chuckled, his eye suggestively roaming over the silk and satin negligees and peignoirs strewn around the room.

"Mmm. This one," he decreed, picking up a sleek blue night shift that was translucent as water. "I feel I've already seen you in it. That day we went skinny-dipping at the spring.''

Mallory colored. In the corner, someone tittered. "Chase! The designer from Vousarre is here!"

"Oops. Sorry." Chase nodded apologetically to the woman as boyish guilt reddened his features.

The woman rose. "Ach, what a man! You are the lucky one, Mallory Leatrice, to make your bed with him." The hint of a smile turned her thin lips as she smoothed her graying hair. "I must speak with your father for a few minutes, if I may? And you, I see, must speak with your man."

"Of course," Mallory said graciously. She waited until the woman exited the drawing room, then turned to find Chase experimenting with the elastic on a sheer pair of panties. "Chase! What are you doing now?"

He grinned. "I'm remembering the first time you unpacked your suitcase, and all these little things just spilled out all over. It was my first intimate moment with you. Only you didn't know it."

Mallory got a catch in her throat, remembering her first impression of Chase's home. The man was impossibly wonderful. What could she say? "But I didn't want you to see any of my nightwear," she pouted, feigning disappointment. "Not now. Not till after the wedding."

"Aw, honey." He threw a comforting arm around her. "It doesn't matter. I'd feel the same way even if you weren't decked out in all these fancy little things."

Decked out in fancy little things. She adored the way he put words together, she'd never tire of hearing him talk. "Say it again," she requested.

"I said, I got it all worked out," he continued, unaware of what she really meant. "Bob will be only too glad to winter at the ranch. So we can winter here, where you can spend time working on your projects for the children's summer camps and be close to your father. Then we can spend summers in Wyoming to keep an eye out for Lewt and the boys.''

"Oh…'' She didn't care a bit about where they lived, she only wanted to hear Chase say he loved her again. She was dissolving into one of those women who longed to hear honeyed words and declarations of love. She was almost disgusted with herself. Yet the way Chase said it was so hopelessly romantic.

He looked at her curiously. "I thought that was what you wanted.''

"It is. Of course.''

"Your father says he's putting things in place so that his business will practically run itself. But if you think you need to be here year-round for that, or him—''

"No, no. It's not that…''

"I told him, Mallory, that I'd work with him—or you—in the shipping industry if it comes to that. But I've got everything I'll ever need. I'm not marrying you for that.''

"I know. I've always known that.''

"Call it pride, but I had to make sure your father knew I loved you, and that's the only reason I'm marrying you. Not his business. Not his status, not your high-society stuff.''

She raised her eyebrows a fraction of an inch. "Wait. Nothing about my life appeals to you?''

He hesitated. "Well, yes. There is one thing.'' A second slipped away as he considered. "The kids' camp. When I saw what you'd done with it I realized this was something I needed, too. It rejuvenates me. I hope you'll let me work with you. I'll feel like I'm doing something for you—and something for Skylar's memory, too.''

Mallory warmed, pleased he could share his feelings

about Skylar with her. "Of course you'll work with me. I'd like that, and we'll find a way to do something special in Skylar's memory. But, I—" Mallory hesitated not wanting to undermine his sincerity, his confidence "—I meant about the other part."

He frowned, obviously confused.

"About…how you didn't care about my trousseau."

"Oh, it's pretty nice," he allowed in his engaging Wyoming style. "But I wouldn't make too much of an investment in it," he warned. "'Cause you won't be wearing it for long."

She bit her lip and offered up a shy, conciliatory smile before she looked away. "No," she said finally, "that's not what I meant, either."

His hold on her tightened, and he sobered. "What're you asking?"

"Are you sure you want to get married, Chase? Truly? Are you sure this is what you want? Sometimes I think this all happened so fast. Are you sure you want to live away from Wyoming? Are you sure you realize the responsibilities that will go with our life here in Narwhal? Or with the kids' camp?"

"Mallory Leatrice Chevalle," he chided. "I'm sure about everything. Why, there's not a horse on this place that could drag me to the altar if I didn't want to go."

They were married in the glen, next to the spring, in a small private affair. Mallory rode with her father to the ceremony in a white wedding carriage. Peggy Sue and her partner attended them, draped in wreaths of laurel and wildflowers. The stable boys, it was learned later, had had quite a time braiding the white ribbons in the black stallion's mane, until Peggy Sue fixed him with a pointed stare.

Bob stood up as Chase's best man. Lewt, Tony and Gabe

were right behind him. It made one side of the altar appear a bit lopsided, but it seemed right, to have them all there like that.

After Chase and Mallory exchanged their vows, musicians from Narwhal's noted harpist colony played the traditional wedding song. During the reception, however, the couple requested the orchestra play upbeat but haunting versions of "Wildfire" and "A Horse With No Name."

"Look at that," Chase marveled, pointing with his champagne glass when the song ended, "I'd swear that Peggy Sue just winked at her boyfriend."

"She probably did," Mallory replied, offering him a bite of wedding cake. "I never realized what a flirt she was. Sometimes it's almost shameful the way she carries on with him."

Chase ate a huge bite of cake and just smiled all the way around it.

The wedding feast was served outside, on long, white-linen-covered tables. Wine flowed from a fountain; beside it was a cooler of longnecks. Cook created a colossal cake, and when they weren't teasing the upstairs maid, Tony and Gabe made bets on whether or not the cake would eventually list to one side. Lewt was too busy explaining to Mallory's father, Hewitt, his strategy for five-card stud. It was a merry time, this coming together of families and traditions—and it lasted for hours.

"Do we dare make our exit?" Chase said impatiently, glancing for the umpteenth time at his watch. "I mean, it was a really nice party, but I'd like a little time alone with my bride." He trailed a suggestive fingertip down the fifty satin-covered buttons on Mallory's back.

She shivered, then took his hand. "Let's say goodnight," she proposed, leading him over to her father. "Father, the wedding and the excitement has wearied us. Thank you for everything.''

He chuckled, knowingly. "You leave us so soon?" Before they could make excuses, he waved them away. "The wedding breakfast begins at ten. Do not," he warned, chuckling again, "lie abed."

Though she was flushed with embarrassment from his insinuation, Mallory kissed his cheek. Chase shook his hand.

"You are a good man, Chase," he said. "I should thank you for making my daughter a happy woman. Now you must gift me with grandchildren before I am too old to enjoy them. It is a charge I put to you."

"Father!" Mallory gasped.

"Ach, go off with you. Go along now. I have dancing to do."

Chase and Mallory faded into the shadows and momentarily watched their wedding party dance by the firelight, near the warm, bubbling spring. He kissed her then, under the spreading branches of a linden tree, and they strolled alone, beneath the full moon, back to the mansion.

The back hall was mysteriously quiet when they slipped inside. The lights were dimmed, but there was a candle in every window. "I feel as if I have the whole house to myself," she said. "Everyone is at the wedding celebration."

"Ah, well, then let's make the most of it," Chase growled, turning her in his arms for yet another sizzling kiss. She clung to him, the full skirt of her gown enveloping them both. "In America," he whispered, nuzzling her ear, "I would have carried you over the threshold. Now I must wait until we are in Wyoming to do it."

"You won't forget?"

"Never." They went up the back stairway, pausing on

every other step to draw out their longing with another sultry kiss. His hand started working the buttons on the back of her dress. "Just trying to get a head start," he whispered.

In the upstairs hall, they slipped into a small nook, where exquisite nudes carved from marble stood on pedestals. "I've always wanted…to do this…here," he said, pressing hot, breathless kisses against her throat, her shoulders. "Every time I pass that beautiful woman…I think of you…in the spring…so innocent and carefree…and—"

"In love," Mallory supplied recklessly, tracing the shell of his ear with her tongue.

He didn't reply, and Mallory was vaguely aware of it. But his palms spanned her waist, and his hands moved up to stroke the underside of her breast. Giddy with anticipation, she quivered. He ran his thumbs down the seams at the side of her gown, while his tongue flicked a kiss in the cleft of her breasts. Mallory felt her body lift, as if it had a will of its own. She stood on her tiptoes to put herself closer to him, and finally Chase put the heel of his hand to one straining tip of her breast and applied the slightest of pressure. He made a circular motion, and his fingertips clasped her fullness, stroking, caressing her through her sequined bodice.

Mallory whimpered as if he'd scorched her through the satin and lace; her head fell back as she involuntarily arched. Chase supported the small of her back and kissed her, tracing wet paths over the tops of her breasts and gently nibbling the delicate flesh. He pushed the neckline of her gown down and nearly exposed the reddened taut bud. The tip of his tongue darted out to seek it. But it was no use, Mallory was virtually cinched inside her gown.

Just enough to tempt, not enough to taste.

"C'mon," he said huskily, pulling away for a second painful time, "we have a marriage to make."

They fled to her suite, both pausing long enough to smile when they saw the sheets were turned down and red rose petals were strewn across them. Champagne chilled in the ice bucket, chocolates were arranged on a silver tray.

Chase scooped one chocolate up and fed it to her. "They say chocolate is an aphrodisiac," he whispered.

She rolled the candy to the inside of her cheek. "In Narwhalian, that word would be...?"

He chuckled. "It's gonna make you want to love me."

She gazed at him, barely conscious of the dissolving chocolate. "Oh, dear. I love you too much already."

He pushed a bit of tulle from her veil off of her bare shoulder, adjusting it. "I think that's a wonderful way to start married life," he said softly. "Us both wanting each other so much we can barely stand it."

They stared at each other for a moment, each one embracing one last moment of private thought before they shared the most intimate beginning of their life together.

Mallory started to remove her veil. But Chase stopped her, taking her hands away, so he could carefully ease the combs from her hair. Then he pulled the pins out of her upswept hair and rubbed the silkiness of it between his forefinger and thumb before letting it tumble around her shoulders. "I've always loved your hair," he said, "from the first minute I saw you. All windblown and wild, as you rode in that convertible."

She smiled, remembering, then turned her back for him to work the remaining buttons on her gown. "Saying things like that will make me vain, and conscious about myself now."

He chuckled. "Do you know," he confessed, working a button at the middle of her back, "that when we ride, I intentionally let you ride ahead of me? Just so that I can see you toss your head and see your hair sweep over your shoulders. Just so I can watch you and see how beautiful you are."

Mallory self-consciously dipped her head.

"It's true. Sometimes I feel like I have to memorize all these things about you so I'll never lose them, so I can keep them with me always. Life is so fragile, Mallory, so fleeting. I don't want to waste a second of it with you."

"Chase…?"

"Yes?"

"When we said our wedding vows today—" at her back, Chase's working fingers stilled "—I said all the words. Like *love* and *cherish* and *honor*. But I kept wondering how to tell you I loved you with my whole heart. It is as if you have become a part of me. I breathe for you. Without seeing you, I *feel* you beside me. How can that be? Sometimes I feel so full with loving you I can barely stand still for the joy of it."

Hearing her admission, Chase's eyes drifted closed. He lowered his head slowly to press a warm kiss on her nape. Inside, he offered up a prayer of thanksgiving.

"Will it always be like this?" she pressed.

His breath skimmed her bare shoulder. "I suspect—between us—it will be that, and more. Every moment, every memory we share will be one more reason to love each other."

For several moments, they were silent, in awe of the magnificence of their first night together. The upstairs hall clock sounded, chiming out the half hour. A cool breeze billowed through the sheer curtains framing the French doors to the balcony and stirred the scent of the rose petals on the bed.

"This dress is a bother for someone who's in a hurry," Mallory said finally, apologetically.

"Who's in a hurry? We have a lifetime." Chase slowly turned the buttons, until he exposed the curve of her lower back, then the tuck of her waist and, finally, the flare of her hips. "Of course, this is ridiculously painful, too. Seeing you inch by inch like this is driving the Wyoming side of this cowboy loco."

"Loco?"

He chuckled. "An expression. Like crazy. You're driving me crazy."

Mallory laughed, and reached beneath her skirt to unzip the underskirt. Then she slipped the gown and the frothy slips over her hips. Stepping out of it, she turned into Chase's waiting arms.

She wore a lacy bra and silk panties and the sexiest of white, thigh-high stockings.

Chase shook his head approvingly, then picked her up and laid her on the waiting bed. He playfully kissed her toes, before hooking a forefinger beneath the elastic of her stockings, to peel one away. His thumb trailed the inside of her opposite thigh, where she was damp and warm with need.

He did exactly the same with the other stocking, then discarded them both beside the bed. Shouldering out of the dark formal western jacket he'd chosen for the occasion, he leaned over her. She started unbuttoning his shirt, working the studs on the front.

When the shirt was open, Mallory buried her head between the sides of cloth to press kisses against his hard, muscled flesh. She sought the wound where Peggy Sue had kicked him.

"I said a long time ago you could kiss it and make it

better," he whispered, yanking off his shirt while she worked his belt and the closure on his trousers.

Somehow their clothes disappeared, and Mallory was left, skin to skin, with her lover, her mate, her husband. He touched her secret places and she discovered his. It was beautiful and comforting, and they were raised to a hazy, rose-colored level of sensuality.

His mouth sought her breast, and he laved at the taut pink bud.

Her fingertips trailed down his torso, exploring the smooth skin of his belly. He guided her hands to his manhood, to let her discover and thrill to the differences of their gender.

"I don't want to hurt you," he said when their need went beyond caresses and kisses. Still, he settled on top of her, adjusting his weight and pinning himself between her thighs, resting against her abdomen.

She wiggled beneath him, writhing to put herself to his advantage. "I want you. It doesn't matter. It will only be once."

"But it is this first time, this one time that will bind us together for eternity." He stroked carefully, tentatively, teasingly. When she was moist and relaxed, he entered her with a single thrust, and she recoiled, arching. "It's okay, baby, it's okay." He held her, and let her grow and adjust to him. She trembled and he lifted her, cradling her in his arms. "I love you," he whispered.

A tight coil of apprehension *snapped* and his love filtered through her, warming with its own heady sensation.

Mallory groaned and he rocked, letting her lose the pain and discover raw, hot pleasure.

Guiding her to the peak of desire, Mallory crashed in tumultuous waves against him. Chase held himself taut, then exploded inside her. She shuddered in his arms, as aftershocks of pleasure rippled through her.

He held her long after she drifted off to sleep, and he wondered, vaguely, if he was a stronger man or a weaker one because of this woman.

It didn't matter, really. Because he was a fulfilled one. And he was fulfilled because of her. He had come halfway round the world to find the one woman who made him whole. And he had no regrets. Not a one. He would spend the rest of his life loving her.

Mallory turned in the circle of Chase's arm. "Did you hear that?" she said sleepily, nudging him.

"Mmm. What?"

"Peggy Sue. She hasn't come by the house so early in the morning for weeks."

Chase squinted at his watch. It was the only thing he still had on. "It's five-thirty in the morning."

"Let's get up," she said, pulling the sheet off of him and around herself.

"Now?"

"Mmm-hmm. Then we'll have time to…you know."

He arched a disbelieving eyebrow at her. "You ought to be sore."

"Me? I'm in good shape."

The most delectable smile turned his lips. "I know."

"Chase!" She blushed at the compliment, then made a show of going to the balcony. "Look. There she is! And the stallion is with her."

Chase rolled out of bed and grabbed a towel to cinch around his middle. "They're something, aren't they?" he said, shaking his head. "I don't think I've ever seen anything so beautiful in my whole life—" he gently slapped her bottom "—present company excepted, of course."

"Chase—"

"Hush." He wound his arms around her middle, pressing her back to his front. "Look at them. They're showing off for us." Both animals preened and threw their heads. Their wavy manes floating in the breeze, they sidestepped, then reared on their back hooves and pawed the air. They whickered and raced into the meadow, Peggy Sue sprinting far ahead of her mate.

"She's such a unique animal," Mallory said finally, "but with such an ordinary name."

Chase cocked his head to the side. "Peggy Sue?" He suddenly laughed. "It's really *not* her name. Skylar named her Pegasus, after a story I'd read her about the mythical, winged horse, but she couldn't pronounce it, so we shortened it to something she could manage. Strange, I'd forgotten all about it." He paused, growing serious, melancholy. "Apparently, life and the legend has come full circle. And it's just going to continue."

"No. There is no more to the legend, Chase."

"Ah, but there is." His cheek was against hers, and she could actually feel him grin. "Babies," he announced.

"Babies?" Her hand immediately went to her abdomen. She supposed it was true. Life could be growing inside her. They had, after all, had a very intimate, very busy wedding night. "I—I guess I wasn't thinking along those lines."

He chuckled. "No, I wasn't thinking of *us*," he emphasized. "But Peggy Sue's in foal. You couldn't tell?"

Mallory glanced quickly back at the speck of white fleeing to the hills of Narwhal. Peggy Sue was going to be a mama. Imagine that.

"Good timing, too," Chase continued. "Won't be long until another Chevalle Cornelle is romping in the hallowed meadow, eh? Probably with our kids. Why, you know, I'll bet we'll just have a passel of kids." He paused and gave her a tight squeeze. "To make your father happy, of course."

Mallory listened, and a smile tugged at her heart. "Of course. We have so much to do, Chase," she whispered, thinking of it, "and so much loving to do to get there." She turned and looped her arms around his neck. "I never really thought about being a mother or having a baby until I knew you. Did you know that?"

"And now?"

"Now I think it would be the most important job in the world."

"I want to have another child. With you," he said, his voice thick. "Someday."

"Someday," she repeated.

They stood in the early morning silence, letting the first warm rays of sunshine tickle their bare feet and penetrate their shoulders.

"I love you," she ventured, her voice quavering. "I have waited a lifetime to say the words, and now I find they are so big I can hardly bear them. You have become my everything, Chase Wells. You are my workmate, my soul mate."

"You forgot something," he teased, whisking his lips over her temple and down to her ear. "Your playmate?" he suggested.

"Yes. Always that…"

He gave her a deep, exploring kiss—one that reached down to their very souls. "I love you, Mallory," he whispered, "and I'll cherish you forever. You have brought me infinite joy. You have made me believe things I never believed possible."

"The legend?"

"No—" he shook his head "—more than that. That I

could risk my heart and love. That I could risk loving someone as special as you.''

"If we have a son," Mallory mused, leaning into him, "I think we should call him Chance."

Chase tilted his head to scuff his chin over the top of Mallory's head. "Because…?"

"Because we took a chance on each other," Mallory explained, proudly using one of her learned American expressions.

Chase chuckled. "Now, remember, that's a Wyoming name, honey. But it's one I approve of especially for our baby boy."

They looked out over the open meadow, growing silent as they watched the unicorn frolic, then disappear to the glen they revered. It had been a long journey, but it had brought all of them home. Love would grow in their hearts…as it would in all the hearts of those who believed.

* * * * *

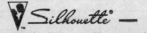

COMING NEXT MONTH

#1630 THE WOLF'S SURRENDER—Sandra Steffen
The Coltons
Kelly Madison had been the bane of the Honorable Grey Colton's existence. Now the feisty defense attorney was back in town, in his courtroom…and ready to give birth! Grey helped deliver her baby—and, to his surprise, softened toward the single mom. But would his ambitions drive him up the legal ladder—or into Kelly's arms?

#1631 LIONHEARTED—Diana Palmer
Long, Tall Texans
Inexperienced debutante Janie Brewster had been chasing successful rancher Leo Hart for years—but he only saw her as a child. At a friend's suggestion, she set out to prove herself a bona fide cowgirl. But would her rough-and-tumble image be enough to win over a sexy, stubborn Hart?

#1632 GUESS WHO'S COMING FOR CHRISTMAS?—Cara Colter
Beth Cavell promised her orphaned nephew snow for Christmas—then handsome Scrooge Riley Keenan appeared and threatened all her plans.
When an unexpected storm forced them to spend the holiday together, Beth wondered if Riley could grant Jamie's other Christmas wish—a new daddy!

#1633 THE MARQUIS AND THE MOTHER-TO-BE—Valerie Parv
The Carramer Legacy
The Marquis of Merrisand might be royalty, but that didn't mean that he could claim Carissa Day's lodge as his own! Except that it *was* his, and Carissa was the victim of a con man. A true gentleman, would Eduard de Marigny open his home—and his heart—to the pregnant temptress?

#1634 THE BILLIONAIRE BORROWS A BRIDE—Myrna Mackenzie
The Wedding Auction
Wanting no part of romance, Spencer Fairfield hired Kate Ryerson to pose as his fiancée—after all, Kate supposedly had a fiancé of her own so there would be no expectations. But his ruse wasn't working the way he'd planned, and soon Spencer discovered the only man Kate did have in her life—was himself!

#1635 THE DOCTOR'S PREGNANT PROPOSAL—Donna Clayton
The Thunder Clan
Devastatingly handsome Grey Thunder wasn't interested in a real marriage—but he *was* interested in a pretend one! Marrying the emotionally scarred doctor was the perfect solution to pregnant Lori Young's problems. But could their tentative yet passionate bond help them face the pain of their pasts?

SRCNM1102